UNDER THE COVERS

MONTANA MAVERICKS
BOOK TWO

REBECCA ZANETTI

This one is for Debbie English Smith, my younger sister, whose gift with horses would've made her fit right in with the Maverick Montana folks. We just returned from an awesome time in Vegas, and according to the Top Dollar machine, "You're a Winner!"

A SPECIAL THANK YOU

I want to extend my heartfelt thanks to Cathie Bailey from the Quapaw Tribe for her invaluable insights and thoughtful feedback on my story. Your perspective and generosity in sharing your knowledge enriched the narrative in ways I couldn't have achieved on my own. I'm deeply grateful for the time, care, and expertise you brought to this project, helping ensure the story resonates with authenticity and respect. Thank you for being part of this journey.

CHAPTER 1

*J*uliet tensed the second the outside door clanged shut. So much for her brief reprieve. She turned around and sat on the highest rung of the ladder, her gaze on the hard wooden floor so far below her feet. Paintings still hung on the wall, and she needed to take them down. But first, she had to face the sheriff.

She'd known he'd show up after receiving her e-mail. Nerves jumped in her belly as she waited.

He strode into the main room of the art gallery and brought the scents of male and pine with him. Stopping several feet away, he looked up. "Juliet."

"Sheriff." She took a deep breath, trying to keep her focus on his dark eyes.

But that body deserved a second glance. Tight and packed hard, the sheriff wore faded jeans, a dark button-downed shirt, and a gun at his hip. Black hair swept away from a bronze face with rugged features. Not handsome, but definitely masculine and somehow tough. Years ago, she'd liked tough. Many years ago.

He cocked his head to the side and studied her.

For months, he'd been studying her...that dark gaze probing deep, warming her in places she tried to control. But Quinn Lodge was all about control, and the smirk he gave promised she'd be the one relinquishing it. "Any other woman, I'd be worried about that top rung. Not you, though," he murmured.

She smiled to mask her instant arousal from his gravelly voice and resorted to using a polite tone. "You don't care if I fall?"

"I care. But you won't fall. You're the most graceful person I've ever met. Ever even seen." Admiration and something deeper glimmered in his eyes.

She swallowed. "Thank you. Now perhaps we should get to the arguing part of the evening."

"I'm not going to argue." Stubbornness lined his jaw, at home and natural along the firm length. "Neither are you."

While the words sounded like a peaceful overture, in truth, they were nothing but an order. She clasped her hands together and smoothed down her long skirt. When he used that tone, her panties dampened. If the boys from the private school who'd dubbed her "frigid virgin" could only see her now. "Good, no arguing. We agree."

His grin flashed a dimple in his left cheek, and he shifted his weight. "You're not leaving the gallery."

"Yes, I am." She should not look. She absolutely would not look. But she'd recognized his move when he's shifted his weight...yes. A very impressive bulge filled out the sheriff's worn jeans.

She swallowed, her ears ringing. Her thighs suddenly ached to part.

His eyebrows rose. "Juliet?"

Guilt flashed through her even as her eyes shot up. "Yes?"

His smile was devastating. "Would you like to finally discuss it?"

"Your erection?" The words slipped out before she could think. *Oh God.* She slapped a hand over her mouth.

He laughed, the sound male and free. "Here in the backcountry, ma'am, we prefer the term *hard-on*. But yes, let's discuss the fact that I'm permanently erect around you. Tell me you're finally ready to do something about it."

Her heart bashed against her rib cage. "Like what?" she choked.

"Well now"— he tucked his thumbs in his pockets, his gaze caressing up her legs to her rapidly sharpening nipples—"I've never taken a woman on a ladder before, but the thought does hold possibilities. How flexible are you, darlin'?"

The spit dried up in her mouth, while warmth flowed through the rest of her. He wasn't joking. If she gave the word, he'd be on her. Shock filled her at how badly she wanted the sheriff *on her*. Most men would be at least a little embarrassed by the tented jeans. Not Quinn Lodge. He wanted to explore the idea.

"While I appreciate your offer, I'd prefer we returned to settling the issue of the gallery." Could she sound any less like a spinster from the eighteen hundreds? "I'm unable to pay the rent, and thus, I need to move on." But where? The upcoming art show needed to be held in town, or nobody would attend. While she had no choice but to flee town right after the opening, at least she could leave on a triumphant note.

"I don't need the rent. Let's keep a running total, and after you're hugely successful, you can pay me." He ran a broad hand through his hair. "Stop being impossible."

She wasn't a charity case. Plus, the last person she wanted to owe was the sheriff. The man viewed the world in clear, unequivocal lines, and she lived in the gray area. A fact he could never know.

"I'm sorry, but I'm not taking advantage of you." She lacked funds, and no way would she stick around.

He sighed. "Juliet, I don't need the money."

The words from any other man would've been bragging. Not Quinn. He was merely being nice…and telling the truth. His family owned most of Montana, and he'd invested heavily in real estate. The guy had acquired many properties, including the two-story brick building that had held her gallery for the past few months, since she'd arrived in town.

She sighed. "I'm not owing you."

His chin lowered.

Hers lifted.

A cell phone buzzed from his pocket. He drew it out, frowned at the number, and then looked back up at her. "I, ah, need to take this. Do you mind?"

"No." Darn if his manners didn't make her feel even more uncomfortable.

"Thanks." He lifted the device to his ear. "Lodge here."

He listened and slowly exhaled. "Thank you, Governor." He shook his head. "I don't think so… Yes, I understand what you are saying." Dark eyes rose and warmed as they focused on Juliet's hardened nipples. She'd cross her arms, but why hide? The sheriff didn't seem concerned about the massive erection he still sported., and she could be just as nonchalant as he. She dragged her thoughts back to his ongoing conversation.

"I would, but I already have a date." That dimple flashed again for a longer time. "Yes, I'm seeing someone—Juliet Montgomery. She owns the art gallery in town. Of course she'll be at the dance as well as at the ride. Thank you very much." He slid the phone into his pocket.

Tingles wandered down Juliet's spine. Several of her fantasies regarding the sheriff included being part of his everyday life. Of course, many more centered on his nights. "We're dating?"

"Well now," only a true Montana man could drawl a sentence like that, "how about we reach an agreement?"

She frowned even as her body sprang to attention. Her raging hormones would love to reach an agreement. "I'm not for sale, Quinn."

He lost the smile. "I would never presume you were. Here's the deal—we both need help. How about we assist each other?"

Without knowing the facts, she knew enough to understand this was a bad idea. No matter how many tingles rippled through her abdomen. "Why did you tell the governor we're dating?"

"He tried to fix me up with his niece, and I needed an out. You're my out." A challenge as well as self-effacing humor danced on his face. "How about we date for the next six weeks, just until the election, and you keep the gallery rent-free? You'd really be helping me out."

Quinn was up for reelection for the sheriff's office. She shook her head. "You don't need to play games. Everybody loves you."

"No. The people in the town of Mineral Lake like me. But Maverick County is a large area, and I need the governor's endorsement. The last thing I have time for is campaigning for a job I love when I need to be *doing* that job."

Considering she'd be leaving soon, maybe she should provide him assistance. "You have more money than the governor. Buy some ads."

"I'm not spending money on ads. It's a waste of resources as well as an insult to hardworking people."

"Tell the governor you aren't interested in his niece." Juliet narrowed her gaze. Quinn Lodge didn't kowtow to anybody.

"Refusing the governor is a bad idea." He stalked closer to the ladder. "His niece is Amy Nelson, a woman I briefly dated, and she wanted more. Her daddy is Jocko Nelson, and he's more than willing to spend a fortune backing Miles Lansing for sheriff. My already dating somebody saves my butt, sweetheart."

The last thing she wanted to talk about was his fine butt.

Nor did she want to think about him dating some other woman. "I'm not your solution."

He reached the bottom of the ladder and held up a hand. "Aren't you tired of dancing around this? For the last few months, we've ignored this tension between us."

"That's what responsible adults do." She automatically took his hand to descend.

Electricity danced up her arm from his warm palm.

"Bullshit." He helped her to the hard-tiled floor. "You feel it, too."

Yes, she did, and the crass language actually turned her on. But he didn't know her, and he wouldn't like her if he did. "I've chosen not to act on any temporary attraction." As a tall woman, it truly unnerved her when she needed to tilt her head back to meet his gaze. "How tall are you, anyway?"

He shrugged. "Six four, last time I checked. How about you?"

"Five ten."

He nodded. "Petite. Very petite."

The man was crazy. She tugged her hand free. "I'm not dating you."

"I know. We're pretending." He glanced around at the many paintings on the wall. "Are these from Sophie's new collection?"

"Yes." The man already knew his sister-in-law's paintings adorned the walls.

"Didn't you promise her an impressive performance for the opening of your gallery?"

Oh, guilt would not work. Juliet sighed. "Yes."

"Well, then. This is the only place to have an amazing showing, right?" he asked.

Wasn't that just like a man to go right for the kill? Sophie was Juliet's friend, one of her only friends, and the showing meant a lot to her. "You're not being fair."

He reached out and ran a finger down Juliet's cheek, his gaze following the motion.

Heat flared from his touch, through her breasts, right down between her legs. "Stop," she whispered.

His hand dropped. "I need a pretend girlfriend. You need to keep the gallery open. This is a perfect agreement."

Darn it. Temptation had her glancing around the spectacular space. Three rooms, all containing different types of Western art, made up the gallery. The main room already held most of the paintings created by Sophie Lodge. Rich, oil-based paintings showing life in Maverick County, activities in the small town of Mineral Lake, and the wickedness of Montana weather. The showing would put both Sophie's art and Juliet's gallery on the map just like the C. M. Russell Museum in Great Falls or the National Museum of Wildlife Art in Jackson Hole.

She wanted to be on that map. Perhaps badly enough to make a deal with the sheriff. Plus, she was tired of trying to ignore her attraction to Quinn. Would that attraction explode or fizzle if they spent time together? Frankly, it didn't matter. She had to leave town soon. Why not appease her curiosity? "Okay, but no touching."

"But—"

"No." She pressed her hands on her hips. The man was too dangerous, too tempting. A woman had to keep some control, or Quinn would run wild. No question. "You're creative, and this is your idea. If we pretend to date, you keep your hands off me."

His eyes dropped to an amused, challenging expression. He held out both hands, palms up. "Tell you what. These hands won't touch you until you ask nicely. Very nicely."

"That will never happen," she snapped.

His left eyebrow rose. "I wondered if that red hair came with a temper." Interest darkened his eyes to midnight. "So much passion locked up in such a classy package. I thought so." He leaned into her space. "Be careful, or I'll make you beg."

She almost doubled over from the spike of desire that shot

through her abdomen. How many pairs of high-end panties had she gone through the last month, anyway? "Back away, Sheriff."

He stepped back, as she'd known he would, but the glittering desire in his eyes didn't wane. He glanced at his smartphone. "Give me your cell number in case I can't find you at the gallery."

She shuffled her feet. A cell? Yeah, right. Even if she had the money, they were too easy to trace. "I, ah, don't have one."

Watchful intelligence filled his eyes as he glanced up. A cop's eyes. "Why not?"

"I have not had time to find the right one and choose a plan," she lied.

"Interesting." He slipped the phone into his pocket, turned on the heel of his cowboy boot, and headed for the door. "Be ready at six tomorrow night for the Excel Foundation Fundraiser in Billings. The drive will take us an hour."

All tension disappeared from the room as he left. Well, except for the tension at the base of her neck from the land line phone being silent. It had been ringing for almost a week with nobody being on the other side. Surely a bunch of kids just goofing off, but she couldn't shake the uneasy feeling that kept her up at night. Well, when erotic images of a nude Quinn Lodge weren't haunting her dreams.

She sagged against the ladder as she forced herself to relax. Yeah, right. Pretending to be the sheriff's girlfriend would be anything but relaxing. What in the world had she just done?

༄ ༄ ༄

THE FUNDRAISER WAS LOCATED at the Billings Mountain Hotel, and the grand ballroom sparkled like something out of New York. Chandeliers lined the ceiling, and real crystal decorated the tables.

Juliet willed her nerves to stop jumping.

Just inside the main doors, Sophie Lodge grinned and looked her up and down. "You are gorgeous. Now stop being a chicken. I let you drive in with me earlier so you could avoid Quinn, but your time is up."

Juliet smiled to keep from frowning at her friend. "First of all, we had to come to the city to choose the music for your art show next month. Then, apparently, you needed to shop like you'd won the lottery." It had been fun to shop with a friend again. Although her life had been odd, at one time, she'd had friends all around her. Cool, cultured friends who minded their own business.

Not Sophie. Nobody in the town of Mineral Lake minded their own business. Shopping with Sophie had been more like an inquisition into Juliet's feelings for Quinn.

Sophie flipped her wispy, blond hair over her shoulder. The mass framed her pixie face perfectly. "The menu we chose from the caterer was ideal, too."

Yes, it was. Unfortunately, the deposit for the food included the last dime Juliet owned. Now she had to go through with the sheriff's charade. So much for changing her mind.

Sophie teetered on her heels. "It was nice of the hotel to let us change in one of the guest rooms."

The hair prickled on the back of Juliet's neck. Was somebody watching her? She cased the room, and too many shadows slithered around the corners.

"I really like your dress," Sophie continued chattering.

For goodness' sake. Juliet needed to get a grip. Nobody was watching her. She glanced down at the sparkling green dress she'd brought when she moved to Montana. "I think I should've worn basic black."

"Why?" Sophie smoothed her hands over the blue fabric hugging her hips and the very slight baby bump. She'd wanted a fun pregnancy dress, but at only two months pregnant, everything had been too big. Her dress had spaghetti straps, a cinched waist, and great lines. "We work hard and deserve a break. Every woman should sparkle."

The last thing Juliet wanted to do was stand out. "This was such an incredibly bad idea."

Sophie shrugged and peered at the crowd. "If you ask me, it was about time Quinn made a move."

"Your brother-in-law and I are friends. He needed a date, and I said yes." Maybe she should tell Sophie the whole truth. "Anyway, you look fantastic. Do you still think you're having a girl?"

Sophie looked around and then lowered her voice to a whisper. "Actually, I'm almost certain it's a boy. I don't know why, but I think so. Which would be cool, because we could name him Nathan, after my uncle." She all but beamed. "Plus, Leila thinks she'll have a little brother, and I swear, that kid is psychic sometimes."

"True," Juliet murmured. Leila, Jake's six-year-old daughter from a previous marriage, showed a definite precociousness.

Sophie grinned. "You are so good at changing the subject, aren't you? We were talking about you and my brother-in-law, sheriff hottie." Sophie waved. "There they are."

Juliet turned to spot Quinn standing by Sophie's husband, Jake, by the far bar. The men were dressed in black suits. She swallowed. The sheriff looked amazing, tough and sleek, in the suit. The jacket was unbuttoned and showed a crisp white shirt. Even then, a sense of contained power vibrated around the man. "Oh, my." Juliet steeled her shoulders.

Sophie nodded vigorously. "I know, right? Those Lodge boys clean up nice. Really nice."

"I see the honeymoon isn't over for you," Juliet said.

"Nope." Sophie started to lead the way through the crowd. "We've been married for a whole month now, and I don't think the honeymoon will ever be over."

Happiness all but oozed from the woman, and a pang of

want hit Juliet. What would it be like to have a wonderful husband, a family, and a life without fear? "Please tell me I can drive home with you tonight."

"Nope," Sophie repeated, tossing a grin over her shoulder. "Jake and I are staying at the hotel. I guess you'll have to drive back with Quinn."

Juliet glanced up to discover dark eyes watching her. Her knees trembled, but she gracefully moved between chairs and people on her three-inch heels. While her mother hadn't taught her much, she had taught her how a lady appeared in public. Whether she liked it or not.

Sophie reached Jake first and was instantly captured in a kiss that belonged in private. Juliet ignored them and kept her focus on the sheriff. "Quinn."

He clasped his hands at his back. "You look beautiful. Can I touch you yet?"

She grinned, her heart lightening. How did he know just what to say to make her laugh and relax? "No, but I'm glad you remembered the rules."

He sighed, a woeful frown on his face. "Rules are meant to be broken."

Boy, did she wish he actually meant those words. "You enforce rules...rather sternly, or so I've heard."

"I believe I'm tough but fair." He used air quotes on the adjectives, a smile in his voice.

A round man three inches shorter than Juliet breezed around the bar. "Sounds like a campaign slogan, Sheriff Lodge."

Quinn turned his head and nodded. "Juliet Montgomery, may I introduce Governor Nelson?"

The governor took her hand in his moist one. "It's a pleasure to meet you."

"And you, Governor," she said softly. "Congratulations on getting House Bill 3000 passed. Very impressive."

His wide chest and even wider belly puffed out. "A beautiful woman who follows politics. You're a lucky man, Lodge."

"Yes, I am," Quinn said, his gaze warm on her.

The lights flickered, and the governor released her hand. "Well, I guess it's time to sit down for dinner. I need to make a quick phone call and will meet you at our table." He bustled off.

Quinn stepped close enough for her to smell pine and male, but he didn't touch her. "HB 3000?"

"A new bill allowing Montana residents to trap mountain lions if they're a threat to livestock." She shrugged. "I Googled recent bills before heading into town earlier."

"Googled?" His grin flashed his dimple. "I think I love you."

Her knees trembled with the need to step back. Even though he was kidding, heat slid through her skin. She smoothed her face into calm lines. "That was easy."

His dark eyes narrowed. "Did I upset you?"

"Of course not." Why in the world did he have to be so observant? She had to get away from him. No way could she spend time in his vicinity and keep her secrets. While she hadn't broken any laws in Montana by using a fake name, she had definitely crossed a line or two. Or maybe having fake identification was a crime. But she hadn't used it, so did it count? Of course, the laws she'd broken back home would land her in prison. She hoped to any God who listened that Quinn Lodge wouldn't be the man slamming the jail door shut.

Quinn leaned closer. "What thoughts are flashing so quickly through that pretty head of yours, darlin'?"

She dropped her eyelids to half-mast. "I was just noticing how sexy you are in a suit, Sheriff." If all else fails, flirt.

"Hmmm." He gestured toward a round table in the center of the room. "How about we go sit before I press you to be honest with me?"

Instinctively, she batted her eyelashes. "You're talking in riddles." Turning on her high heel, she sauntered through tables and chairs to reach their spot. Her rear end burned from his gaze, and she couldn't help but glance over her shoulder.

She shouldn't have looked. He stood, his focus on her bare skin, fire in his eyes.

The sheriff wanted her—and he had no intention of hiding it.

Grabbing a chair back, she stopped moving before she fell on her face. This was going to be a long night.

CHAPTER 2

Quinn waited for the bartender to count his change, his gaze on the woman sitting at their table. He'd settled her in her seat before returning to the bar. They had the white wine she liked, and he wanted her happy.

His brother shot him a grin. "Sorry I couldn't ride in with you earlier—my hearing today took longer than I thought."

Quinn had always been proud Jake was such a hotshot lawyer. "No problem."

"I know." Jake eyed the table. "You and Juliet, huh? Finally?"

"Yes."

As usual, Jake went right for the throat. "How?"

Quinn dropped a tip in the jar. "I told her I needed a date, in fact, I needed a girlfriend until the election." Which was the truth. Her sticking by his side would certainly ease the situation with the governor and his niece.

Jake snorted. "Juliet fell for that?"

"So she says." Quinn couldn't stop the wry grin. "She required a push, she's a sweetheart who wants to help, and it seemed to work."

"Maybe she just doesn't want to date you. How many times has she turned you down, anyway?"

"Twenty or so." Quinn lifted a shoulder. "Though she's interested." He frowned and accepted the change. "There's something about her that seems off. Not dangerous, just off."

Jake took a glass of Scotch and an orange juice from the bartender. "I'd run her background."

Yeah, Quinn had thought about a background check. He reached for Juliet's wine and his ginger ale. "I'd rather she told me the truth."

"I get that." Jake turned toward the table. "My daughter is thrilled you're finally out with Juliet because she's ready for a new aunt."

Quinn almost spilled the wine. "I like Juliet and think we'll have some fun. You need to explain things to Leila." Leila was six years old and way too wise for her years, maybe because her mother had passed away when she'd been so young. But she'd found a new mama when Jake married Sophie, and now she wanted everyone married and happy.

His brother kept walking. "Sometimes marriage sneaks up on you. Trust me." He sat next to Sophie and handed her the juice.

Quinn sat. Nothing snuck up on him, and he wasn't the marrying kind. At least, he wouldn't marry until he stopped being a threat to the people around him. While he had his emotions mostly under control, some nights he awoke from a nightmare, thinking he remained in Afghanistan struggling for safety. Until reality set back in.

Juliet reached for her riesling and cut him a quick glance.

Next to her, Amy Nelson chattered on about the summer collection of designer shoes she'd just bought. What was it with women and shoes? She should've spent more money on material for a dress. The white one she wore stretched tight against her ample bust and stopped several inches up from her knees.

Her boobs pushed out of the sides and up the top, and she'd probably have bruises from the fabric cutting in. Her uncle, the governor, sat next to her texting something on his phone. A widower, he'd apparently brought his niece as a date.

Next to him sat Miles Lansing, one of Quinn's two opponents in the sheriff race. Lansing was a politician, not a cop, and he didn't belong with a gun in his hand. His wife, a brunette with hard eyes and a slinky black dress, sat to his left, her gaze appraising.

Quinn glanced at Juliet again. Her green dress clasped at one shoulder, leaving the other one bare and inviting for his mouth. It cinched at her tiny waist and flared down to her feet. Although the sparkles covered most of her, she was sexy as any dream. An Irish sprite in his Montana world. His cock instantly sprang to attention, which was nothing new when Juliet was near. He leaned over to whisper, "You really do look stunning, Juliet."

A sweet blush rose from her neck up over her porcelain skin.

Sophie's head jerked, and she raised an eyebrow at Amy, the expression a woman got when she was about to defend a friend. Quinn rolled back the last few minutes of chatter in his mind. Oh. Amy had made a comment about homespun dresses and Juliet's sparkles. That was a girl insult, right?

He opened his mouth to say something nice about the dress, only to stop when Juliet patted his hand. The innocent touch shot straight to his groin, and he snapped his jaw shut to keep from groaning.

She smiled. "Oh, Amy, you're so sweet. I bought this at Saks in New York last season. They have the nicest personal shoppers in the designer section. You really must give them a try— they're masters at helping women choose the, well, the right size for their figures." She turned toward Sophie. "How is the design for the golf course in North Carolina coming?"

Delight flashed across Sophie's pretty face. Quinn had a

feeling the delight was due to the smack-on insult Juliet had delivered so classily and not from the question about design, but who the hell knew. Women had a language he'd never fully understood, although Juliet had a couple of levels to her he hadn't anticipated. Classy, elegant, and tough. She handled the political situation like she'd done so her whole life. But she came from a small town in Idaho, right?

"I'm almost finished with the practice greens," Sophie said with a grin. Multitalented, Sophie designed golf courses when she wasn't painting masterpieces. Her first art show would take place in a month at Juliet's gallery, and both women seemed to be working hard.

Amy interrupted Sophie, her blue eyes flashing sparks. "When were you in New York, Juliet?"

Juliet took a sip of her wine. "Last year. Every once in a while, I like to visit art collections in the city to see what's new just so our Western art is up to speed at my gallery."

Her hand shook slightly as she set her glass down. Most people wouldn't have noticed.

Quinn Lodge wasn't most people. The woman lied. Why?

He glanced at his brother to see if Jake had noticed, but Jake was busy tracing Sophie's knuckles with his fingers. Damn newlywed. "Jake, how did your hearing go today?" Quinn asked.

Jake lifted his gaze, his expression knowing. Oh yeah, he'd noticed Juliet's discomfort. "Fine. The hearing was just a status conference regarding an upcoming trial. Not nearly as interesting as a good election fight."

"Speaking of campaigning"— Miles looked down his patrician nose—"I find it odd Bennington isn't here tonight."

The governor shrugged. "Perhaps he's not as serious about running for sheriff as the two of you." Faded eyes appraising, the governor surveyed the room.

"He's probably busy running his ranch," Quinn said smoothly. He liked Bennington, but the guy had a fierce temper and shouldn't carry a gun or badge. He should stick to his ranch and the wildness surrounding them all.

"Bennington doesn't have much backing." Miles leaned forward. "I've heard the Kooskia Tribe doesn't support him. Frankly, the tribe only supports its own."

Quinn smiled. "The tribe supports the best person for the job, regardless of tribal affiliations. Always has, always will." Right now, the Kooskia Tribe backed him, and he liked to think it was because he did a fine job. Though he was self-aware enough to know it probably didn't hurt that he was a tribal member and his grandfather the chief.

Miles rubbed his Rolex. "I'm sure you could always get a job with the tribal police force."

"I'm sure I could." Quinn met the man's gaze evenly. "I like collaborating with them and still policing the entire county."

Mile's quick smile promised fierce competition. "Interesting."

Juliet smoothed out her napkin. "Miles, what experience do you have in law enforcement?"

Warmth flooded through Quinn. The pretty redhead had just defended him.

Miles cleared his throat. "I'm more of a financial leader, which we need in the county. Not every sheriff needs to swagger around and shoot people."

Jake snorted. "Have you been swaggering and shooting people again, Quinn?"

"I guess so. Don't tell Mom." Quinn slid his arm around Juliet's chair, careful not to touch. Something in him wanted to tuck her close and hold tight.

Dinner passed quickly and included veiled insults from Amy, classy counters by Juliet, and threats from Lansing about how new blood was needed in the sheriff's office. By the time the waiter removed their dessert plates, Quinn's temples pounded.

Sophie nudged him. "I can't believe you're not drinking," she whispered.

He could use a Scotch. Or three shots of tequila. "I'm driving Juliet home, and I'm on call tonight." Several deputies were out with the flu going around town, and he needed to be alert.

"Bummer." Sophie took a healthy gulp of her orange juice.

Sometimes Quinn wanted to drop his sister-in-law in the lake. At her impish grin, he smiled back. Nah. He adored the pixie-sized smart ass.

An orchestra in the corner started playing softly, and he pushed away from the table, glad for the reprieve. "Juliet? Let's stretch our legs. Please excuse us, folks."

"I'd love to, Sheriff." She rose from the table, all grace, all beauty, and smiled at the group at large. "Thank you for a wonderful dinner. Enjoy the rest of your evening."

The governor patted his round belly. "We'll see you Saturday at the charity ride? It's for the boys home outside of Missoula and is so important to our constituents."

"We'll be there," Miles Lansing said, a smirk on his lips.

Quinn forced a smile. "Juliet and I wouldn't miss it. See you then."

They needed to get away from the table. Quinn followed her as she glided around tables and people to a quiet area by the bar. Tall and curvy, she moved with an intriguing elegance. Her backless dress revealed a sexy spine right down to her tiny waist. Damn, he loved backless dresses. His fingers itched with the need to touch her silky skin, but he'd made a promise.

Juliet stopped, turned, and rested against a three-foot-wide wooden pillar. "Well, dinner was interesting."

His shoulders relaxed for the first time all evening. "Do you understand why I didn't want to escort the governor's niece?"

"Yes. I can't believe you dated her." Juliet's eyes glowed like emeralds in the soft lighting.

"Me either." He glanced over his shoulder to catch their table watching him. He focused back on the stunning woman within his reach. "They're watching us. How about a kiss to convince them we're truly together?"

"We're not." Pink wandered across her high cheekbones. She'd worn her dark red hair up in a sophisticated twist he wanted to tangle. "There's nothing between us, Sheriff. You need to know that."

He loved a good challenge, so he stepped close enough to smell citrus and woman. "I disagree. There's a lot between us, Juliet. Now, how about my kiss?"

❧ ❧ ❧

JULIET HAD SIPPED JUST enough wine, dealt with just enough snide comments from Amy, and fought off enough attraction to the sheriff to pick up the challenge. All night she'd been aware of the heat pouring off the man and of every contained move he made. "You think you can kiss me without touching me?"

"I didn't promise not to touch you. I promised to keep my hands off you." Dare, with more than a hint of male, glittered in his eyes. "One kiss to convince people around us that we're together…and to convince me that you're not interested in me."

She pressed her palms and her back against the smooth wood. For so long, she'd been afraid to date. Most men turned tail and ran when they got to know her. Quinn would never get the chance to desert her because she'd run away first. So why not accept the sexy promise in his challenge? Freedom flushed through her. "All right. Let's see what you've got, Sheriff."

His eyes darkened to a dangerous hue. Slowly, keeping her gaze, he put both hands on the pillar on either side of her head, effectively caging her.

The breath caught in her throat. Desire hummed awake in her abdomen. The world silenced around her, narrowing to the man suddenly in her space.

He leaned forward until his lips hovered over hers. "Close your eyes." The words brushed against her skin in a soft but unmistakable order.

Her eyelids fluttered closed. For seconds, nothing happened. Then a firm glide of warm lips brushed hers, and she opened her mouth with a sigh. He slanted his mouth and deepened the kiss, all male, all in control. Her head was trapped, her body secured, and his mouth gave no mercy. Gentleness slid into possessiveness. He kissed her hard enough she could do nothing but take all he was giving.

Electricity zipped from her lips to her breasts, zinging around until sparking between her legs.

Her nails dug into the wood in an effort to remain still. Then her hands moved on their own and tunneled through his dark hair, like she'd wanted to do for months.

His tongue brushed hers, rubbing on the roof of her mouth. With a soft groan, she slid her hands over his broad chest to clutch his hair. Her nipples pebbled harder than diamonds when she pressed her body against his. Her clit jumped to life, pounding with a need so great it actually hurt.

He went deeper, making her head spin.

She forgot where she was. For the first time in months, she forgot who she was. As he kissed her, she could do nothing but feel.

For eons, she remained lost in the whirlwind created by Quinn Lodge.

Slowly, he softened the kiss. Finally, he released her mouth.

She gaped at him, her hands in his thick hair, her body pressed against his. *Oh, oh.* She blinked several times and released him to lean back against the pillar. His hands remained flattened against the wall. He'd kept his promise and hadn't touched her. Of course, she'd almost tackled him to the ground to ride like a prized pony.

Expecting triumph on his face, she stilled at the genuine pleasure lighting his eyes.

His cheek creased. "Juliet, I do believe you're one of a kind."

Kindness from the sexy man would be her undoing. She'd tell him to go away...if her voice worked. There was no way her voice worked. What should she do?

His dark gaze dropped to her throbbing lips. "Why did you lie during dinner?"

Alarm flared through her mind with the clanging of bells. "I didn't lie."

His gaze rose to pin her as effectively as his lips had a moment ago. "Yes, you did. While I couldn't care less why or when you went to New York, I do care that you lied to me."

Then he shouldn't have asked her to be his date. She'd been lying to him since day one, which was why they had to stay apart from each other. The sheriff noticed everything. "I don't know what you're talking about, and I really don't appreciate being questioned like this."

"My apologies." His jaw firmed. "Are you in trouble? I mean, do you need help?"

Yes, she was in trouble, mainly from the sexy sheriff. "No."

He sighed. "This isn't one of those situations where you're running from debts, the law, or an abusive ex-husband, is it?"

Close, but not quite. "I give you my word I'm not running from debts, the law, or an abusive ex-husband." It was the truth, and by the way his body relaxed, he believed her.

"Okay." His hands dropped away from the pillar. "Can I touch you yet?"

She smiled, her body roaring with need. If she gave in to it, he'd burn her up. But it might just be worth it. "I'm not interested."

His upper lip quirked. "Darlin' I could have you coming around my cock in three seconds, and you know it."

The rough tone and crass words almost sent her into an

orgasm right there. Never in her life had she been talked to in such a manner—who knew she'd enjoy it? Or maybe she just liked Quinn. "You're terribly confident, aren't you?"

"Want me to prove it to you?"

Yes. Definitely yes. She lifted her chin and glanced around the ballroom. "Where? A nice linen closet somewhere?" Her sniff held just the right amount of derision to darken his eyes.

He leaned in, his heated mouth on her neck. "When I take you for the first time, and believe me, it's going to happen, I want a bed and all night. You're going to scream my name, and you're going to beg, pretty Juliet."

It was a good thing she hadn't worn panties. Why bother? As his confident tone wrapped around them, so did reality. She was leaving, and for the first time, she wondered if she had the power to hurt him. Hurting Quinn was the last thing she wanted to do. "You made a promise—no touching," she whispered.

He levered back, gaze narrowing on her. Whatever he saw made him lean back more. "You're all stubborn Irish, aren't you?"

"Close enough," she murmured.

He nodded. "Okay. You get your reprieve for now. Let's go have a drink next door with Jake and Soph, and then I'll take you home. Tomorrow I work, but on Saturday, I accepted an invitation for us to ride in the Boys Club trail-ride."

Panic heated her. "Ride? Ride what?"

His left eyebrow rose. "Horses. Of course. Why?"

She swallowed. "I, ah, I don't ride."

He blinked. Twice. "What do you mean?"

"I don't ride horses. Ever." How hard was that to understand?

"That's impossible. You're from Idaho, right?" He cocked his head to the side.

What did that have to do anything? "Ah, yes," she lied, keeping her gaze open and on his.

"But you don't ride."

She shook her head. "No. Never have."

He slowly nodded, his eyes narrowing. "Okay. I get off work at four tomorrow. Meet me at my house, and we'll go for a quick lesson."

"No way," she blurted out.

"You live in Montana, sweetheart. Sometimes nature makes it difficult to get around, and you need to know how to ride a horse."

By the set of his stubborn jaw, he would not back down. The last thing she wanted to do was pique his curiosity. If he ran a background check on her, she was in for a world of trouble. "Okay. Fine."

Her on a horse. Quinn Lodge being curious. Things were going south...and fast.

CHAPTER 3

The following morning after discovering pretty Juliet couldn't ride a horse, Quinn glanced in the rearview mirror of his truck. "Is your seat belt secure?"

Leila rolled her eyes, looking young and innocent with pink ribbons at the end of her braids. "Uncle Quinn, I put the belt on right away. Are you going to marry Juliet?"

The questions had been peppered at him for the last five minutes as he drove through town. "No. Is the belt tight?"

Dark eyes met his in the mirror. Aware and intelligent eyes. "I axed you a question."

He swallowed. "I answered your question."

"Don't you like Juliet?"

"I like her just fine." In fact, after dropping her at home the previous night, it was all he could do not to break down her door and take another kiss. They'd had a nice drive home, and while she'd been mostly quiet, the silence had been comfortable. But sometimes a situation required finesse. Juliet deserved space, and for a moment in the ballroom, she'd seemed afraid. He couldn't let her fear him, so he'd backed off. Of course, he'd see her for the riding lesson at his ranch later that afternoon.

He drove the truck away from the main hub of Mineral Lake, heading for a development outside of town, and focusing back on his niece. "I'm not getting married. Juliet and I are just friends."

"Nuh-uh. You always look like you wanna kiss her when we talk about her." Leila tugged on her pink sweatshirt.

He coughed. "I do not."

"Do too." Leila glanced out the window. "Daddy looks at Mom that way." A small flush wandered over her tiny features. "Sophie says I can call her mom. That's okay, right?"

His heart warmed until his chest hurt. "I think it's great, little one. Sophie is a good mom to you."

Leila shrugged and watched the trees flying by outside.

Quinn slowed the truck to turn into the subdivision. The poor kid only had pictures to remember her mother since she'd died when Leila was just a baby. "I remember your mom as someone who loved you with all her heart. She would like you to have Sophie as a mom now, sweetie. This would make your mom happy."

Hope filled Leila's eyes when she turned toward him. "You promise?"

His heart might just break. "I promise. Your mom would want you happy, right?"

"Yes," she whispered.

"This is a good thing. Love is always a good thing." He waited until she nodded, relief filling her face. Then he turned between stone pillars forming the entryway to the subdivision.

"If you love Juliet, that's a good thing then," Leila said.

There was no way he would win that debate. He grabbed a silver star from the empty ashtray and handed it over the seat. "You are hereby deputized again to assist me in official sheriff duties."

"Cool." Leila grasped the star and pinned it to her chest. "I'm your favoriest deputy, right?"

"Without question." Though the girl would eventually find a safe career in her adult life, if he had anything to say about it. Chances were, he didn't. "I need you to keep Mrs. Rush company while I talk to her son." He stopped the truck in front of a newly painted blue house, stepped out, and assisted Leila to the ground.

"I know." She hopped happily next to him, her braids flopping. In her dark jeans, pink shirt, and scuffed tennis shoes, she was the most adorable deputy he'd ever seen. Her black eyes and hair were all Jake, but her delicate bone structure came from her grandmother.

They rang the bell, and Anabella Rush opened the door. Her blond hair was mussed and her eyes tired, but the grin she flashed reminded him of the sweet girl he'd kissed behind the bleachers at fifteen. She hoisted a three-month-old baby to her shoulder, tottering only slightly in the boot cast covering her right foot. "Thanks for coming."

"No problem." Quinn followed her inside the house and stepped over a stuffed bear, three toy trains, and a baby's binkie on the way to the back door. "How many kids do you have now, anyway?"

She laughed. "Very funny. Considering you're godfather to all of them, you know we only have three. It just seems like twenty." Sighing, she patted the baby's back. "I swear, every time Charlie comes home on leave, we end up having another one." Sliding open the glass door, she stepped lightly down four cement steps and over a tricycle before pointing to one of several large trees fronting federal forest land. "Henry is up toward the top."

Quinn glanced down at her. "How did you hurt your foot?"

"I tripped over the tricycle." She chuckled.

"I'm glad you called." Quinn nodded at Leila. "My deputy will take your statement, while I go, ah, climb a tree."

He left the ladies talking on the porch and crossed the wide lawn before arriving at the heavy birch tree. Looking up, he sighed. The kid sat far up, only one dangling tennis shoe in sight. Quinn seized a sturdy branch and hauled himself up. Branch after branch, he climbed upward, bark scraping his hands and faded jeans. Finally, he reached Henry.

"Hi," Henry said, shoving his glasses back up his nose.

"Hi." Quinn found a heavy branch and sat, making sure the eight-year-old sat on a secure and strong branch. He seemed fine. "Why are you in a tree?"

"I was thinkin'."

Quinn surveyed the area, smiling as he caught Mineral Lake in the distance. Mountains rose tall and strong around them, while the valley spread out with ranches and homes. "This is a good place to think."

"Yeah." Henry coughed. "My mom called the cops, huh?"

"Ladies don't like when people climb trees and they can't climb up to make sure everything's all right," Quinn said.

Henry rolled his eyes, the blue flashing behind thick glasses. "Dude, my mom can climb a tree. Well, usually."

"That's Sheriff Dude to you, buddy," Quinn said.

Henry snorted. "I heard you're going to marry the art lady."

Quinn stilled. "Where the heck did you hear that?"

"Baseball tryouts." Henry frowned and kicked out a skinny leg.

"I see." Quinn rubbed his chin. "How did tryouts go?"

"Not so good." Henry bit his lip. "Yesterday was warm-up day. Tryouts are actually next week."

Quinn nodded. "I guess tryouts are kinda hard with your dad being overseas, huh?"

"Yeah. He's down range of Afghanistan again." Henry hunched narrow shoulders. "He was supposed to teach me how to throw a curveball, but he had to go…"

Oh, man. "So you're in a tree thinking about the situation?" Quinn asked.

"Yeah. Seemed like a good place to think," Henry mused.

"Why didn't you call me?" Quinn asked.

"I figured you were busy catching bad guys and chasing the art lady," Henry whispered.

Regret slammed into Quinn's gut. "I'm never too busy for you. I played baseball through high school and then college football. I can toss a curveball." He kept his voice calm, while he yelled at himself inside. He should've been checking closer on his friend's family. "Plus, my younger brother, Colton, was the best pitcher in the state for years. It's May, and he's home for summer break from graduate school. We'll get him over here this afternoon."

Hope filled Henry's face. "Really?"

"Of course." Quinn held his hand up for a high five. "Now, let's go get down and make sure your mom isn't mad at us for being in the tree so long."

"Okay." Henry flushed and rubbed a hand through his spiky hair. "That's not the only reason I'm up here."

Quinn settled back down. *God, please don't let it be a sex question.* He wasn't ready for that, but he had offered to help, so he'd figure something out. "You can talk to me about anything. What's up?"

Henry pointed to the wide yard next door. "I was watching Mr. Pearson, just making sure he's okay."

Quinn slowly turned his head to spot a naked, ninety-year-old man plucking weeds away from his fence. "He's naked."

"Yeah." Henry sighed. "He's been making moonshine in the shed again, and sometimes he samples the goods. Today, I think he sampled the goods."

Quinn strangled on a cough. "Does your mom know he makes moonshine?"

"Nope. She really doesn't climb trees very often." Henry grabbed a branch and started descending. "Do you hafta arrest Mr. Pearson?"

"I at least need to talk to him." Quinn stepped gingerly on a narrow branch.

"Okay. But you gotta know, he'll run. He likes to run sometimes," Henry warned.

Wonderful. Quinn shook his head. He actually wanted to fight for the sheriff position again? As he glanced at the now whistling, stark-nude old guy, he grinned. Yeah. Why the hell not?

JULIET SLOWLY APPROACHED THE PADDOCK, wondering how in the world she'd ended up in this particular mess. Sophie had been kind enough to drop her off at Quinn's ranch house, but at some point, Juliet needed a car. Though licensing a vehicle under a fake name would be too risky, and she really didn't want to break the law any more than she probably already had.

She rubbed her aching eyes. She'd had a sleepless night after the sheriff had dropped her off after the ball, and her exhaustion was all his fault. The kiss had her body on fire and her mind whirling.

Plus, when she'd gotten up to get a drink of water, she could've sworn somebody tapped on the outside door to her apartment. She'd pressed her ear against it, no way stupid enough to open it, but nothing.

The ranch smelled like the wild outdoors with pine, huckleberries, and dust. The barn door opened, and the cause of her restlessness stalked out, leading two saddled horses. Today the sheriff wore dark jeans and a long-sleeved T-shirt that hugged his fine muscles like it had been crafted from horny female cotton.

He tipped his black hat up on his forehead.

Desire slammed through her so quickly she stopped moving.

The Stetson shadowed his angled face in a way promising danger and sex, and not necessarily in that order.

She swallowed. "Those are big horses." The biggest one, all black with wild eyes, loomed large. A stallion? The second, a light tan with a dark brown mane, stood still nearby. Though much smaller than the other one, it remained enormous.

Quinn rubbed the shadow on his jaw. "I've dreamed about you wearing tight jeans. My dreams didn't come close to the reality."

Serious and intense, his deep voice wandered right down her belly to pool in heat. Was it possible to be seduced by a voice? She squared her shoulders. "Why did you chase a naked old man around the Maverick subdivision earlier today?"

Quinn chortled and handed her the reins to the smaller horse. "There are no secrets in Maverick, now are there?"

That wasn't true. Not even close. She frowned at the quiet animal. "No."

Quinn leaned close and brushed a kiss on her forehead. "It's nice to see you, Juliet."

She nodded, her tongue suddenly thick.

His eyes darkened. Keeping his hands on the reins, he tilted his head and his mouth captured hers. Firm and warm, his lips tempted her until she opened for him.

She could've easily stepped back.

Instead, she stepped forward into the heat generated by the man.

He deepened the kiss, taking her under, making her head spin. Finally, he released her and focused on her face. "I've wanted to do that since our kiss last night."

Juliet breathed deep, trying to dispel the crazy need rushing through her body. Her throat dried up, making speaking impossible.

"This is going somewhere, Juliet," he said.

Panic shoved desire out of the way. She shook her head.

Amusement filtered through his eyes. "Apparently you need time. That's all right. I'm a very patient man."

She glanced around the area in a lame effort to control her libido. His sprawling ranch house held a wide porch, the colors matching the three closest barns. Acreage spread out in every direction, some fields, some trees, plenty of cattle in the far distance. "I like your place."

"Me too." He smiled. "Mom and Tom live toward the north, while Jake and Sophie have a house to the east of here. Apparently Colt wants to build over that way, as well."

"You've combined all the family ranches?" she asked. What would it be like to have family you actually wanted to be around?

"Sure. We all work the cattle and share the profits—and losses." He shrugged. "Are you done stalling?"

She swallowed. "Yes."

He chuckled and drew the smaller horse closer. "This is Moona, and she's a sweet mare. I borrowed her from Jake. Put your foot in the stirrup, and I'll hoist you up."

Juliet cleared her throat and tried to ignore her still-humming abdomen. Man, the sheriff could kiss. "I can get up." She'd seen this done on television.

"Sweetheart, let me help." Charming was too tame of a word to describe his smile, and the deepening of his voice turned the tone unbelievably sexy. "Just a quick caveat to the no-touching-rule limited to helping you on and off the horse. I promise."

Either she could make a fool of herself and fall on her head or let the sheriff assist her. "Fine."

Quinn grasped her waist and swung her onto the horse. Her butt hit the leather saddle. He instantly released her. Ignoring the heated imprint from his hands, she wiggled into a comfortable position.

"Excellent." Smooth and graceful, the sheriff hoisted into his own saddle. "You've ridden a little, right?"

She considered lying. He had probably been riding since birth, and he'd figure out the truth. "No. This is my first time."

"How is that possible?" he asked.

"My folks owned a store in Idaho, and we lived in town. No horses." This time she did lie and kept her gaze on the mare's mane. The sheriff needed to quit probing into her past. "Tell me about the naked man you arrested."

"Just a minor arrest for public nudity and being drunk on moonshine," Quinn said. "He made bail, and I took him back home."

Just what she'd thought. "You couldn't give the guy a break?"

"I had to make sure he had a good meal." One dark eyebrow rose. "Plus, the guy broke the law."

No wiggle room with the sheriff and his values. He would never understand why somebody might need to break the law, and she needed to forget this crazy crush she had on him. "You're a hard man, Sheriff."

"So I've been told, darlin'." He held the reins and easily controlled the massive beast. "Are you all right on the mare?"

Besides still being horribly aroused and sitting on a wild creature of death, sure, she was fantastic. "I'm fine."

His gaze lowered to check the stirrups. "You're a delicate one, Juliet Montgomery. I want you to go slow and take it easy. If you get scared, we stop."

A hard man with a sweet side. A very intriguing, sweet side. Juliet couldn't bring trouble down on him. If the truth about her family came out, just being linked with her might hurt him professionally. "I'm not delicate."

"Yes, you are. But I won't let anything hurt you. I promise." He flashed an encouraging smile. "You can do this."

She came from the city where predators wore fancy suits and drove fast cars. In Montana, the strong wore cowboy hats and didn't care about the rest. Without a question, Quinn Lodge held a natural toughness no city man could match—but he played fair. Those who played fair got hurt. She couldn't allow for him to get hurt from knowing her, because her family *never* played fair. "This isn't a good idea, Quinn."

"Sure it is. Just use your hands and legs to steer Moona. She's easy," he said.

Had he really misunderstood her? Taking a deep breath, Juliet nudged the horse with her knees. The animal trotted forward.

Ack. Juliet grabbed the reins tighter. She bit her lip while her rear end hit the leather saddle. Slap. Slap. Slap.

Pain ricocheted up her spine.

She whimpered, her mind rushing to the inevitability of her flying over the horse's head and landing on her face. Panic shot through her. Yanking up on the reins, she kicked her feet.

The horse shot into a gallop, straight for the solid ranch house. Juliet screamed, her body flying into the air and slamming back on the saddle.

A low expletive echoed behind her before Quinn snapped an order to the horse. The animal halted immediately. Juliet lunged forward onto the pommel and dropped back. Safely.

She hissed out a breath. Her butt ached already.

The sheriff jumped off his horse and strode toward her. The sun slanted across his strong face, highlighting his Native American features in a way she hadn't caught before. Such purposeful steps from such a dangerous man made her want to kick the horse again just to get out of his path.

He reached up and grabbed her elbows, pulling her off the beast. Two seconds later, she stood on the unmoving, rocky, very safe ground. Her legs wobbled as she took several deep breaths.

The mare whinnied and wandered toward some tall grass.

Quinn released her, tipped back his hat, and grasped the reins of his stallion. "I've never seen anybody move exactly the opposite of the horse, before." Shaking his head, he quickly untied his saddle and tossed it on the ground but left the heavy blanket in place. The black horse snorted and twitched its tail.

She stepped away from the monster. "I told you I couldn't ride."

"I know." Quinn's hands circled her waist.

"No." She shook her head and attempted to evade him.

He kept her in place. "Trust me." With a mere shift of his massive shoulders, he tossed her onto the huge stallion.

CHAPTER 4

*P*anic heated Juliet's blood. He'd thrown her on top of a wild stallion. She grabbed the silky mane. "What in the world?"

Planting both hands behind her butt, the sheriff jumped up behind her.

Heat fired down her torso. Desire unfurled inside her with the strength of a tornado. Sparks flew throughout her skin. Instant and unexpected.

He leaned forward, his breath whispering against her ear. "Now relax."

Her nipples hardened to points. Fuzziness filled her mind. A need ripped through her veins so demanding she could barely breathe.

The horse huffed.

Strong, large hands settled into the mane in front of her.

On all that was impossible and holy. She bit back a whimper that wanted loose.

"Okay." His heated breath caressed her ear. His hard chest cradled her back. "Tighten your legs, and you can control the animal."

She swallowed. "I, uh..." Her voice lowered to a huskiness she barely recognized.

"You're safe." His voice slid to guttural.

She tightened her grip. "Okay. What now?"

"Just click your tongue and pull in with your foot," Quinn murmured.

His heated breath licked around her ear, brushing her face, shooting beneath her skin to warm her. Everywhere. Her eyelids fluttered. Thank goodness he couldn't see her face. Mentally smacking herself, she kicked the horse.

The animal snorted.

Quinn leaned into her, his hardness cradling her back. He dug his boot into the horse's flank, man and beast both rippling with impressive strength.

The horse moved forward.

Flutters that had nothing to do with fear rippled through Juliet's abdomen. She sucked in air scented with male. Her eyelids became heavy, while her limbs tingled. Her breasts ached. Her sex softened.

"Okay. Now you steer him." Quinn's voice dropped to the tenor of gravel in a cement mixer.

This type of instant desire was unreal. Couldn't be happening. A long shiver wandered down her entire body. He had to have felt it.

"Juliet." He groaned.

Naturally, unwillingly, her head dropped back to his chest. "Quinn."

He stilled and then exhaled. "Juliet, you need to concentrate."

"Can't." Desire reduced her to one syllable, and she couldn't find it in herself to care.

Muscles vibrated against her back. "What do you want, darlin'?"

She groaned low in her throat and shut her eyes. "Quinn."

"Juliet, either start paying attention to the lesson, or tell me what you want."

What did she want? Him. Without question, him. It was a mistake, one she'd probably regret, yet one she wanted to make so badly. "I want you."

He stiffened. The breeze wandered around them with the scents of honeysuckle and pine. "Say the words," he said.

If she said the words, there would be no going back. She'd definitely have to leave town after the art showing. It was only a matter of time anyway. "Touch me."

Sharp teeth nipped her ear, spiraling hunger inside her veins. "Ask nicely."

Her eyes flashed open. His dominant tone trembled through her nerves, sparking around her body until lighting her skin on fire. "Please."

His hand flattened against her stomach, and he pulled her into heat and male. He chuckled, the sound heavy with need. With a slight shrug that moved her shoulders, he slid his palm up to cup one breast over her shirt. "Finally."

Electricity zinged from her chest straight to her clit. A roaring filled her ears. "Don't stop."

He tweaked her nipple, and she exhaled on a sob. How was it possible to be so in need?

Spring sunshine cascaded down, and they sat on a horse in front of his house. Anybody might come by and see them. The summer day radiated warmth, but still, she shivered. She struggled to regain a sense of reality. "We're outside."

"I know." He grasped her shirt and ripped it open, sending buttons flying. Warm hands cupped her bra-covered breasts before he flicked open the front clasp, freeing her. A low groan rumbled from his chest as one rough palm caressed her.

He grasped her chin and tugged her head to the side, exposing her neck. Leaning down, he scraped his teeth along her jugular, kissing and nipping along the way.

He tugged on her nipple.

She arched into his hold, her mind spinning. "Quinn—"

Jeans rustled as he swung his leg and jumped from the horse. Grabbing her waist, he pulled her off, pressing her against the horse's flank until she wrapped her legs around his hips.

His mouth took hers.

Hot, fast, crazy, he kissed every thought out of her brain while pivoting and striding toward the house. His boots clomped up the steps, and at the porch, he released her to slide down his body. The entire time, he kept kissing her.

She grabbed his shirt and broke the kiss so she could yank the material over his head. He helped her, his mouth back on hers the second they succeeded. His lips were firm, determined, and he deepened his assault until all she could do was kiss him back.

Vaguely, she heard the clasp of her jeans release. Cool air brushed her bare butt as he pulled them off along with her boots, socks, and underwear.

They shuffled closer to the door, and she grabbed his jeans.

He released her mouth. "Wait."

"No." She shoved his jeans down his legs, taking a quick moment to gasp at the heavy cock straining toward her.

Wow. The sheriff was built.

The jeans caught on his boots. Oh well. She could see what she needed. Slowly standing, she brushed a kiss across his impressive shaft on her way back up.

A low growl rumbled from him.

Both hands clasped her shoulders, and he slid her shirt and bra off. Red spiraled across his rugged cheekbones, and his nostrils flared. "We need to slow down."

"No." She stepped right into heat and male. His broad chest showed a warrior's scars. While she'd heard he had been in the service, she hadn't known he'd been in battle. Defined and muscular, his chest led down to an impressive six-pack. His erection brushed her stomach, and she had to fight to keep from moaning in need. "Please don't treat me like I'm some sort of fragile lady. I'm not."

"You are," he said.

No, she never had been. No matter how badly she'd disappointed her family. Leaning forward, she licked his nipple.

His sharp intake of breath made her smile.

"Quinn, we do this right. Like you want." She lifted her gaze to meet his. Tingles zinged around her from the raw hunger on his dark face.

"Like I want?" he asked, his voice guttural as he shoved open the door and propelled them inside.

"Yes," she breathed out, her heart pounding.

"I need to run upstairs—"

She shook her head. "I'm on the pill—medical reasons."

His eyes flared hot and bright. He kicked the door shut and backed her against the wall. Both hands plunged into her hair, and he took her mouth again. They inched along the wall, hopefully toward a bedroom. She should probably help him out of his boots and jeans so he didn't trip. The wall disappeared, and only cool air ran along her back.

She moaned into the kiss, her body on fire. "Now, Quinn. Please, now." The hunger was so great, she was about to drop him to the floor and take him.

With dangerous grace, he flipped her around, his hand heavy against her lower back. She had a second to appreciate a comfortable-looking dining room complete with hutch. A thick table hit her upper thighs, and she bent over, her torso over the table and him behind her. He shoved papers to the side that cascaded to the floor.

Manacling both her hips, he gently began to ease inside her.

Whoa. The sheriff was huge. She closed her eyes and willed her body to relax around him. His control was impressive, as he went inch by inch, obviously trying not to hurt her.

She held her breath, her body rioting. "Hurry up, Quinn."

"Hold on," he groaned, finally pushing all the way in.

Sparks flashed behind her eyes, and then she opened them in shock. Pinned against the table, helpless, she breathed out, her nerves firing. So much demand coursed through her, she could barely think.

"You okay?" he rumbled, the hands on her hips tightening.

"Yes," she whispered. She'd never felt like this—never—but that was something to worry about later. After. Way after. Going purely on instinct, she wiggled her butt. "More."

His grip turned brutal. Pulling out, and then shoving back in, he began to pound. Hard, fast, so strong, he thrust. The sound of flesh slapping flesh echoed around the room.

Flames licked inside her sex right where he plunged, filling her almost too full. She clapped her hands against the table, her body straining for release.

Somehow, he increased the strength of his thrusts, propelling her up on her toes. Each relentless drive sent her higher. Her thighs trembled and started to shake. Her sex contracted until pain and pleasure melded together.

A ball of fire exploded inside her, spiraling out through nerves, muscles, and skin. She arched her back and cried out, her eyes closing. Waves of sparking pleasure whipped through her in shattering spasms.

The orgasm lasted forever. Finally, the waves ebbed. Coming down, her body relaxing, she rested her cheek on the cool table.

His fingers left bruises as he ground against her while he came.

She felt the second reality returned to him. His hold relaxed, and whiskers rubbed her neck.

"Juliet?" he asked.

"Hmmm." Opening her eyes and speaking real words would be too much effort. She'd quite possibly never felt this good. Ever.

He withdrew from her body and gently lifted her off the table. Then he turned her around to face him. "Sweetheart? You okay?"

Her eyelids slowly opened. Concern bracketed Quinn's handsome face and glowed bright in his gaze. She managed a tired grin. "I'm excellent."

He shook his head. "I was too rough."

Reaching up, she ran her palm along his jawline. "You were perfect, Quinn Lodge."

His shoulders relaxed. "That was only round one, sweetheart. Now we get serious—in the bedroom. Where I can treat you right." An expression filtered into his eyes she couldn't identify. Warm and soft, it increased her heartbeat and set alarm bells ringing in her head.

She swallowed, wanting to protest.

He leaned down, the room tilted, and she found herself cradled in his arms. He headed out of the dining room. She snuggled close, enjoying the sensation of muscles shifting in his chest as he moved. Wasn't there something—

Reality hit them both at the same time. Quinn stopped suddenly with a sharp intake of breath.

The jeans were still around his boots.

His eyes widened, he tried to hop, but whatever had tripped him wasn't letting go. The room swirled around.

Juliet yelped and dug her nails into his chest.

He spun midair, changed their positions, and dropped backward onto a coffee table. She landed hard on his chest. For a heartbeat, the room silenced. Then the table gave way. Wood splintered with a resounding crack, and they crashed to the floor. She smacked her head on his chin. He groaned.

Frowning, she rubbed her head while settling on top of him, straddling him. "Are you all right?"

He exhaled, and a table leg rolled out from under his rib

cage. "Yes." Both hands ran down her arms. "Are you all right? Did I hurt you? I'm sorry, Juliet."

Warmth flushed through her. "You sacrificed your body for me."

He grimaced. "I like your body better than mine." His hands wandered from her arms to play with her breasts. "Are these okay?"

Heat climbed into her face. Electricity zapped from his fingers to her rapidly awakening core. "Ah, fine."

"Good." His voice roughened. "Though I should check you head to toe in order to make sure. Once we're in the bedroom."

The world disappeared. "Now that sounds like a smart plan." Her worries, her fears...everything except the sexy sheriff ceased to matter. For this one stolen moment in time, life was good. No matter what happened the next day, she wanted this night. Pushing against his impressive chest, she scrambled over his already erect cock and down his legs. "Let's get your boots off first."

"Good idea." He sat up, and pieces of the table rattled.

She huffed out a laugh and yanked off his boots along with his jeans. "There, now. No more tripping."

He shoved himself to stand and kicked the jeans out of the way. They spiraled through the room and hit a Western oil painting on the far wall. The painting dropped to the floor.

Juliet covered her mouth with her hand. "There'll be nothing left of your house when we're done."

His grin was all wolf. "Works for me." Lunging for her, he ducked a shoulder and tossed her over it.

She caught her breath at his speed, her face against his back. He began moving through the house. A calloused hand caressed her butt, and she wiggled. He caressed harder, taking claim, holding her in place.

A tingle wandered through her.

He climbed stairs, and his fingers dipped between her legs.

She gasped out, seeing stars.

Slowly, one finger entered her while another tapped her clit. She gave a strangled cry. "No, stop."

He stopped moving just inside a doorway. "Okay." Another finger slid inside, stretching her.

Oh God. "I meant—"

"I know what you meant." His silky hair brushed her skin, and his teeth nipped her thigh. His thumbnail scraped across her clit. "Control isn't something you get to keep here, Juliet."

Her abdomen quivered. If he didn't cease his playing, she was going to orgasm over his shoulder, completely at his mercy. While the idea was intriguing, she had to keep some dignity. "Being upside down gives me a headache."

His fingers deserted her, and she had just enough time to relax before a hard slap echoed across her buttocks. Fire lanced straight to her sex. "Quinn." She meant it as a protest, but his name came out on a moan.

"No lying—not here and not now. When we're like this, only honesty. Agree or you go home." His muscled shoulders shifted as he took a deep breath. "After I turn your ass red."

She gasped and then slowly relaxed. Lies didn't belong between them when they were together like this. "No lying," she murmured. Then, her hands slid down his back to grab a very impressive ass. "Though I'm getting bored with this discussion."

He laughed and took several steps. Air brushed her skin as he laid her on a bed. His fingers trailed down her abdomen. She gyrated against him, her breath catching.

He released her, and she tensed in protest.

"We have time, sweetheart." Desire spiraled high across his face. Grabbing her hips, he pushed her up the mattress, his body covering hers. He brushed the hair away from her forehead. "You're beautiful."

She blinked. This was about sex. Great sex. She couldn't offer more. "Quinn, I—"

"Shh." He nipped her lips. "I know. No worries."

Well, that might hurt a little. "Oh, okay."

He settled between her legs. "But for the next couple of hours, you're mine."

The possessive tone battered down any defenses she'd been trying to shore. "Maybe I'll claim you, Sheriff." Tangling her fingers through his thick hair, she tugged his mouth down to hers for a slow, long, drugging kiss.

A jangle echoed by the doorway. "Freeze!" a woman yelled.

Then things happened too fast and too slow all at once.

Juliet screamed.

Quinn leaped from the bed and toward danger.

Juliet scrambled beneath the bedclothes.

"Jesus Christ," Quinn bellowed, jumping back for the bed and shoving under the covers with her.

Juliet clutched the bedspread to her chest, her gaze on the doorway. Quinn's college-aged sister stood with a bat clutched in her hands, her blue eyes wide, and her face extremely pale.

The woman's mouth opened and closed several times. She threw the bat to the floor and ground her fists into her eyes. "Oh my God, oh my God, oh my God. I could've lived my *whole* life without seeing...*that!*"

Quinn threw a pillow at her while remaining safely covered. "What the hell are you doing here?"

Dawn ducked the pillow and peered between two fingers. "I wanted to talk to you and found Moona wandering down the road. Titan followed right behind her."

"Oh." Quinn sat up but kept the bedspread over the important parts.

"And"— Dawn's voice rose in pitch and volume as she dropped her hand— "I walked inside and it looked like a big fight had taken place. The table is broken, a painting is down, and I heard a noise up here. So, I grabbed the bat and came upstairs."

Quinn stilled. Tension vibrated through the room. "Let me get this straight. You noticed signs of a fight, of danger, and your logical choice was to grab a bat and come upstairs."

"Um—" Dawn took a step back.

Juliet fought the urge to hide her face under the bedspread. "I'm so sorry, Dawn."

The woman shuffled her feet. "No, I'm sorry. I didn't know— I mean, that you and Quinn—well, I mean—"

"Go away," Quinn muttered. Then he frowned. "Why didn't you call for help before coming upstairs?"

Dawn's eyes widened just as heavy boots pounded up the stairs. Jake rushed into the room followed by Colton, their younger brother. Both men wore faded jeans, work gloves, and thick shirts. They'd obviously been working the ranch.

Dawn giggled. "I did call for help."

Oh, no. Heat shot into Juliet's face so quickly her skin burned. She pulled the sheet over her head.

Jake's laugh rang through the room.

"I'm going to arrest all three of you for trespass if you don't get out of here," Quinn barked.

The sound of a door closing was a prelude for a moment of silence before laughter echoed down the hallway stairs. Quinn tugged on the sheet.

Juliet held onto the heavy cotton with all of her might.

"Juliet? They're gone," he said, amusement in his voice.

It didn't matter. She'd never live the last few moments down. Good thing she was leaving town. Soon.

CHAPTER 5

*J*uliet settled more comfortably on the kitchen chair, her gaze on the half-naked warrior cooking dinner. "I think we may have blinded your sister for life."

Quinn chuckled and stirred the scrambled eggs. "I'd prefer not to think about it again." The muscles in his impressive arms shifted as he reached for salt and pepper to dump on the eggs. He wore scars on his back, and it hurt she wouldn't have time to get close enough to ask about them. But she had the night, and she would enjoy what she could. He'd thrown on jeans but had left his torso and feet bare. Very masculine. "If I hadn't been nude, I probably would've smashed both Jake's and Colton's heads together for not leaving right away." While the words emerged tough, obvious affection lived in them.

"You and your siblings seem close." Juliet picked at a loose thread on the shirt she'd borrowed.

"We are." Quinn removed the pan and slid eggs onto two plates. Delivering one to her, he grabbed a plate of buttered toast. "You don't have siblings?"

"No." Not really, anyway. She eyed the eggs. "These look fantastic."

"Thanks." He sat and tossed her a napkin. "Eggs are the only thing I know how to cook. Well, besides Christmas cookies."

Juliet unfolded the napkin on her lap. "Christmas cookies?"

He grinned. "Yeah. Leila and I have a tradition of making Christmas cookies shaped like sheriff stars every year. It's our, ah, thing."

Talk about the sweetest thing Juliet had ever heard. "You're a softy, Sheriff."

"Humph." He dug into his eggs. "Why the gallery, Juliet?"

She paused. "What do you mean?"

"The gallery? There are tons of businesses you could open, and you choose a Western art gallery in a small Montana town. Why?" Lazy intelligence glimmered in his eyes.

The need to confide in him surprised a grin out of her. "I love art. Love paintings, drawings, sculptures—even comic books. No matter how hard I tried, I never had talent." She took a sip of water. "Skill, maybe. But not the talent so few have that amazes anyone who looks."

He nodded. "So you decided to surround yourself with art."

"Exactly." For the first time in a month, her shoulders relaxed. "I do have a good head for business, and I have an eye for other people's talent. That works."

"Do you still paint?" he asked.

"No, but I do sculpt once in a while. Just for me, and just for fun." Her pieces were more functional than inspirational, but that was okay.

The phone rang, and he stretched over his head to grab the handset off the wall. "Lodge." He listened for a moment and then stood to look at his cell phone sitting on the table. "Yes, Mrs. Romano. I understand. Give me a minute." He set down the handset and punched in a number on the cell phone.

Juliet tilted her head to the side. What in the world was going on?

Quinn waited and smiled. "Hi, Mrs. Maceberry. This is

Sheriff Lodge, and I could use Graham's help. Is your son home?" Quinn glanced at Juliet and winked.

Sexy and strong, that wink shot right down to throb between her legs. The man should be captured on film.

"Graham?" Quinn straightened up. "Mrs. Romano's cat is stuck in the tree down the street. I owe you lunch next week if you go and get the darn thing down." Quinn nodded. "You're the best, kid. Be careful and don't fall." The cell phone clicked shut. He lifted the handset to his head. "Mrs. Romano? Graham Maceberry has become my official cat catcher. He'll be there in a few minutes to get Snookie down. Just offer the kid one of your amazing strawberry scones when he succeeds. Yes, ma'am. Have a good night."

With a sigh, Quinn dropped back into his seat. "My job's a dangerous one, darlin'." The smug grin sliding across his face promised both danger and sin.

"I can see that." She licked cheese off her fork.

His eyes flared.

She stopped licking. "Don't look at me like that."

"Like what?" he asked.

"Like you want to eat me alive." She paused as heat filled her face. "You know what I mean."

"I know exactly what you mean." He'd leaned forward to say something that had to be sexy when the doorbell rang. He frowned. "What is up with people today?" Tossing his napkin on the table, he strode into the other room. Voices echoed, and he returned with a plate full of brownies and a casserole dish covered with tinfoil.

Juliet lifted her eyebrows.

Quinn smiled and shoved the plates into the refrigerator. "Mrs. Phillips is missing both of her sons. One is in Idaho at a convention, and the other is overseas. She always makes plenty of food, and I usually get extras when the boys are out of town."

Juliet glanced past him to the myriad of different dishes in the refrigerator. "It looks like a lot of women feed you."

"Yeah, I guess." He shut the door and retook his seat.

She'd bet her last pair of shoes most of the dishes were made by single women and not grandmotherly types like Mrs. Phillips. "Well, a man has to eat something other than scrambled eggs and cheese."

"Exactly." His gaze wandered over the white dress shirt she'd borrowed. "You look darn nice in my shirt." He shoved his plate to the side. "Why don't we head back to bed?"

She swallowed, caught by the fire in his eyes. "Good idea."

The phone rang again. With a muffled expletive, Quinn answered it. After listening, he took a deep breath. "I'll be right there." Hanging up, he flashed an apologetic grin. "Joan Daniels heard a noise in her backyard. She called me because she's just down the road, and I can get there sooner than the guys on duty in town."

Juliet studied his strong face. "You don't seem worried."

"She hears something every other week or so. It's usually the wind. But, we did have a sighting of a cougar last week, so I need to check it out." He reached for his gun on top of the refrigerator. "Can I borrow that shirt?"

"No." Juliet slid off the chair. Forty-year-old, four times divorced, Joan Daniels wore low-cut shirts and partied in town a lot. *She* was the cougar Quinn should look out for. No doubt she'd called the sexy sheriff for more than a cougar sighting. "I'll clean up while you're gone."

"You're the best." He placed a quick kiss on Juliet's forehead. "I'll make it up to you when I get back." After running upstairs, he returned fully dressed and wearing his hat. "Lock the door behind me." Then he was gone.

How many women did the sheriff rush out to rescue on a daily basis? Juliet shook her head. She didn't have a claim on the man, and she'd insisted on no strings. A quick survey of the kitchen proved the sheriff made quite the mess when he cooked. But hey, he had cooked for her. She dug in and had the room cleaned in short order. The silence ticked around her.

Maneuvering up the stairs, she made the bed. Sitting down, she pressed the sheriff's pillow to her face. Male, wild and free. Yeah. The scent of Quinn. The sense of safety surrounded her in his bed. With a sigh, she lay down and closed her eyes for just a moment.

A strong hand shook her shoulder. "Juliet? Wake up, baby."

She started awake.

Quinn stood over her, lines of fatigue cutting into the side of his mouth. "It's after midnight. I'll take you home before heading to the station to write up my report."

She shook her head and sat up. "Was there something outside of Joan's house?"

"Yes. A fully grown, hungry cougar." Quinn rubbed his whiskered jaw. "Now we have cougars too close to residences. Those animals can be wicked."

"Oh." She flipped back the bedspread and stood. When had she fallen asleep?

Quinn tugged her into his hard body and rubbed his chin on the top of her head. "Thank you for a wonderful night."

"Right back at you, Sheriff." The warm arms around her melted her muscles into relaxation.

He stepped back. "Get dressed, and I'll meet you downstairs. Also, Sophie is driving up to the lodge instead of riding in the trail fundraiser tomorrow. I'll have her pick you up on the way so we don't risk putting you on a horse again—at least until I can give you more lessons."

His idea of lessons warmed her entire body. She cleared her throat. "I appreciate Sophie giving me a ride." That way, appearances would be met. The world would see them as a couple. Well, they were having sex, but he didn't want her to stay the night. That was all right. She didn't want to sleep over, now did she? Yeah, maybe she wouldn't mind cuddling with his hard body for a while. Hurt spiraled through her, and she pushed the feeling away. "I'll be ready in a moment."

He nodded and headed downstairs.

Well, now. Where exactly had she left her clothes?

CHAPTER 6

The morning sun trickled weakly through the heavy clouds, promising a rainstorm. Quinn wound twine around the post, snipping the ends into smoothness. The heated summer-storm season would soon hit, and the ranch wasn't prepared. "You're lucky I didn't have my gun on me last night," he muttered at his brother.

Colton chortled and kicked a rock into place to secure another post. "From what I saw, you didn't have anything on you."

Quinn threw the ball of twine at the dumbass. "You're a moron."

"Maybe." Colton tugged his Stetson down against the piercing wind. Even so, his multicolored hair blew around his neck. "But I would've kept the woman all night and not driven her home before midnight."

Jake glanced up from where he pounded in a new post.

Irritation whipped through Quinn stronger than the wind. "I haven't kicked your ass in a while, little brother, but don't think I'm opposed to the idea."

The smart-ass grin Colton shot him nearly guaranteed a

beating. "Sounds like fun. I haven't just been studying animal science, accounting, and finance the last three years, you know."

"Don't think the MMA crap you've been doing comes close to special-ops training, Colton Freeze." Sure, Quinn was proud of his little brother. That didn't mean he couldn't beat the shit out of him now and then.

Jake threw the hammer into the back of the battered Ford where it clanked across the faded metal. "I'm fairly certain the sheriff shouldn't commit battery—especially during an election cycle."

"Stop sounding like a lawyer," Quinn snapped.

"I am a lawyer." Jake grabbed a fence-hole digger and drove the blades into the moist earth. "As much as it pains me to admit this, I agree with Colt. Your reputation of lovin' 'em and leavin' 'em is ticking off Mom. Let a woman stay the night once in a while."

"Love 'em and leave 'em?" Quinn hefted a fence pole from the back of the truck. "I don't even date anybody in town."

"You don't date, period." Colton moved out of the way for Quinn to shove the pole in the ground. "You have sex and leave. Unfortunately, the city isn't far away from our small town, and everybody knows your cycle."

Jake angled around and grabbed part of the pole to plunge down. "I think Mom has Tom geared up to talk to you. Just a heads-up."

Quinn groaned. While he loved his stepfather and appreciated him becoming a father to Jake and him when they were young, he didn't need a fatherly talk about sex. "Tom has enough to worry about with Dawn." The youngest of them all, little Dawn was plain wild...and in love with the wrong man. "We all have enough to worry about with Dawn."

Colton shoveled dirt around the post. "Nah. The last time Hawk came home on leave, they didn't even talk to each other. She's over him."

Quinn cut his eyes to Jake, who shrugged. "That would be excellent news." Not that he didn't like Hawk, because he did. They'd all grown up together and were good friends. But Hawk's time in the military weighed heavily on him, and Dawn was way too young to get serious over a man. "What about you, Colton Henry Freeze?"

Colt grinned. "I'm not in love, don't plan on being in love, and am ready to graduate and head home. In fact, I'm going to build over on the east side of the ranch, near the falls."

Quinn yanked his leather glove off to rub his chin. "What about Melanie?"

Jake snorted. "Dumbass here hasn't figured out Mel's a girl."

Colton tossed the post digger onto the truck bed. "Mel's been my best friend since kindergarten. Of course, I know she's a girl."

"And?" Quinn asked.

"And nothin'." Colton jumped to sit on the tailgate. "We're friends. She's dating some banker from Missoula. The guy wears three-piece suits. Three piece." He shook his head.

Colt was a moron when it came to women. But, on the other hand, the place he wanted to build would be perfect for a ranch house. When their mom had married Tom, they'd had Colt and Dawn. When the Lodge boys were old enough to make the decision on their own, they'd combined the Lodge and Freeze acres into one sprawling ranch they all worked. Any profits were split evenly. His biological father had been dead for many years, but Quinn was sure he'd be pleased with how things had turned out. "How is Melanie's grandpop doing?"

Colton shook his head. "Not good. The doctors say he's terminal."

"I'm sorry to hear that." Quinn ripped off his hat to wipe his forehead.

Jake reached for a thermos and poured coffee for all three of them. "Somehow we got off the subject of Casanova here and Juliet Montgomery."

"We're finished with that subject." Quinn took a deep drink of the unloaded brew and grimaced. Another seven months until Sophie's baby was born, damn it. Too lazy to make two pots, Jake had switched them all to decaf until then.

"I know why you either leave or kick a woman out of your bed, Quinn," Jake said quietly.

Of course he knew why. They'd gotten drunk, really drunk, about two years ago and told each other everything they'd seen, everything they'd done, while in service for their country. Then they'd never spoken about it again, which worked just fine for Quinn.

"So do I," Colton murmured.

Quinn narrowed his focus on his brother. *"You* don't."

Colt shrugged. "I may not know the details, but I know you've struggled with PTSD. That's the only thing that would make you kick Juliet Montgomery out of your bed. Period."

Sometimes Quinn forgot his youngest brother was a freakin' genius. Smart as hell, and nothing got past him. "You don't understand."

"I'm not pretending to understand. But, I also know you'd err on the side of caution so as not to hurt somebody, when really you should be taking a chance. That woman is worth the risk." Colton took a gulp.

Jake staggered back. "Did you just get relationship advice from numb-nuts here?"

Colton laughed and jumped from the truck. "I may be younger, and I may not have fought overseas, but you know what? I'm right."

❧ ❧ ❧

JULIET BRUSHED HER HAIR, satisfied with her sparkling-clean apartment. The tiny three-room apartment above the gallery offered both charm and easy maneuverability. She tried not to wriggle on the seat of the vanity in her bedroom.

Her rear end hurt. Mainly from the darn horse ride, but her hips showed slight bruises from the sheriff's grasp.

The thought brought a smile to her face. The man was passionate and explosive, and he'd stopped treating her like glass. Thank goodness.

The phone rang, and her fingers trembled before she answered. Could the sheriff be calling?

A throat cleared. "Um, Juliet?"

She exhaled. "Hi, Sophie. What's up?"

"Um, well, don't freak out, okay?" Sophie said.

Juliet's blood pressure rose. "Okay."

"The good news is that the Western Pacific Art Council is sending dignitaries to the art showing, and if they like the paintings, they'll give us a grant for the gallery," Sophie said, her words rushing together.

Hope bloomed in Juliet's chest. "That's amazing. How did you—"

"The bad news is I told them we could have the showing Saturday in order to meet the deadline for the grant process," Sophie interrupted.

Panic cut off Juliet's breath. She wheezed out. "Saturday is in three days."

"I know, but I've finished all the paintings, and even the charcoals are ready to be hung. We can do this. I promise."

That was crazy. But a grant from the WPAC would guarantee the gallery remained open, even if Juliet had to leave. Sadness compressed her lungs—she thought she'd have more time with Quinn. She sucked in air sprinkled with courage. "Okay. We can do it."

Sophie's happy squeal ripped through the line, and Juliet held the receiver away from her ear. "We need to get to work."

"After the trail ride today, I promise we'll come help you hang the art. We can also send out an email blast and make some flyers for town," Sophie said.

Juliet shook her head, even though nobody could see. "I'm not riding today."

"I know. Quinn asked me to pick you up, and we're on our way now. His mom and I are driving up to the lodge for the picnic. Wasn't that sweet of him?"

"Humph." Yes, it was sweet to get her a ride, and now she could relax. But she remained uncomfortable about the sheriff. "I'll be outside in a few minutes." After saying good-bye and hanging up the phone, Juliet finished with her makeup. She couldn't leave town until after the showing, but a few days wouldn't make a difference.

The phone rang again, and she rolled her eyes. What bombshell would Sophie ring down now?

"Hello?" Juliet chuckled.

Silence.

"Hello? Sophie?" she said.

More silence. Then something shuffled. Somebody breathed. Heavy and somehow ominous.

Juliet cleared her throat. "If this is Tommy Nelcome, your mother told you to stop making prank calls. I'm calling her right now."

The caller hung up.

Okay. That was just a kid. Nothing to worry about. Though he'd been calling a lot lately. Juliet dialed her neighbor, Judy Nelcome, to rat out Tommy. Unfortunately, Judy reported that Tommy was visiting his grandparents in Oregon, and they'd gone to the ocean for the day. So the caller wasn't Tommy.

Juliet hung up and took several deep breaths. Just because the caller wasn't Tommy didn't rule out another kid goofing off.

She'd been careful, and she was safe. Her family couldn't find her. An illogical and disastrous need filled her to call the sheriff and ask for help.

It was just a prank call, for goodness' sake. Yet another prank call.

She yanked on cowboy boots, pleased they matched her long skirt. Since she didn't have to ride a raging beast, she didn't need to change. After adding several pieces of silver Celtic jewelry, she whipped through the apartment, grabbed her purse and coat, and headed down to the gallery. Tucking her arms in the sleeves, she stepped outside the main door, making sure to secure the locks.

A chilly wind scattered leaves down the quiet street. Their rustling scraped against crumbling asphalt.

The hair on the back of her neck prickled. She glanced at the still storefronts. Her breath burst out in pants. Nobody hid in the shadows. Her mind wanted to play tricks on her from a silly prank phone call. An SUV turned the corner, and she sighed in relief at Sophie in the driver's seat, her blond hair up in a ponytail.

Loni Freeze, Quinn's mother, waved from the passenger seat as they paused by the curb.

Juliet waved back and jumped into the back seat. "Thank you for picking me up."

"Of course. You look lovely today, Juliet," Loni said.

"Thank you." Juliet fought to keep from blushing, considering Loni's son had bent Juliet over a table the other day and made her see stars. "So do you."

Loni smiled. Definitely petite, it was a surprise the woman had birthed and raised three large sons as well as the energetic Dawn. Quinn had inherited her dark eyes and angled Native American features, but his size must've been his father's.

Sophie signaled and pulled into the street. "Sorry about the huge car. I wanted to bring the smaller one, but you know how Jake gets."

"Yes." A pang of jealousy smacked Juliet between the eyes. What would it be like to have an overprotective husband who cared so much? Sophie had been in a car accident a short time ago, and Jake seemed a bit obsessive about ensuring she drove around in something close to a Sherman tank. "This way we get to stretch out, anyway."

Loni laughed and glanced out the window. "A spring storm is coming, but at least we've moved from snow and sleet to just rain. I hope the rain misses the riders today."

Juliet followed her gaze as they drove through an intersection. A black SUV waited at a stop sign, the windows tinted. She focused, seeking the license plate. There wasn't one.

The vehicle pulled onto the road behind them.

CHAPTER 7

*J*uliet kept her eye on Sophie's cell phone, just in case she needed to dial for help. They arrived at the lodge within record time. While Sophie drove a big car, she apparently still believed in speed.

The black SUV had disappeared at the base of the mountain.

Maybe her imagination ran wild. The SUV might've been new, or perhaps a tourist had gotten lost in town. She could find no indication somebody dangerous had been tailing them.

Juliet slipped from the vehicle.

As a unit, Quinn and his brothers stalked out of the cedar-sided lodge. She swallowed. As a force, they commanded notice. All three stood to well over six feet tall, and appeared muscled as well as dangerously graceful. Dressed in faded jeans, long-sleeved shirts, and cowboy boots, they embodied every girl's vision of a bad-boy cowboy. Where Quinn and Jake had dark eyes and hair, Colton had deep blue eyes, and a myriad of colors made up his thick hair.

He grinned and kissed his mom on the cheek. "You're late."

Juliet flushed and shuffled her feet. The last time she'd seen Colton, she'd been naked and hiding under the covers.

He leaned in and brushed her cheek with a brotherly kiss. "Hi, Juliet."

"Hi." Her heart warmed.

"Get away from my woman," Quinn lumbered, a slight grin tipping his lips.

Surprise filtered through Colton's eyes that matched Jake's lifted eyebrows. That was a bit of a claim, now wasn't it? Juliet frowned.

"My brother is right—for once. You look very pretty, Juliet." Quinn stepped into her space. Then he kissed her. In full daylight, in full view of his family, the sheriff grasped her chin and captured her mouth. His lips slanted over hers, while heat cascaded off his hard body. He took her under, exploring, taking his time as if he had every right in the world to do so.

Liquid lava shot through her, and reality disappeared. It came crashing back all too soon. Her hands flattened against his chest and shoved.

He paused and lifted his head. Darker than midnight and just as mysterious, his eyes focused on hers. "Did you just push me?"

The spit in her mouth dried up. She swallowed. "Yes. We're in public."

"I believe that was the deal." His hold tightened imperceptibly on her chin.

She glanced around, sighing in relief that everyone had gone inside. They'd probably hurried just to escape the inappropriate public display of lust. "Well, we're alone now."

"And?" His thumb swept along her jawline.

"We don't need to pretend." Irritation battled with her unwelcome desire. She needed to distance herself from the sheriff before he discovered her secrets. Or broke her rapidly beating heart—he hadn't even wanted her to stay the night after the truly excellent sex.

He frowned, his large frame blocking the weak sun. "What's eating you, darlin'?"

"Nothing." She pushed, and might as well have been trying to shove a cement wall out of the way. "Back off, Sheriff."

He studied her, his gaze serious. "No."

Did he just refuse? Not the polite, follow all the rules, stickler of a sheriff. "Excuse me?" She jerked her head, dislodging his hold.

Her triumph didn't last long. Quinn stepped into her, and her butt hit the car. Trapped. "I. Said. No." He rested a hand against the roof. "We'll stay right here until you tell me what has you tangled up."

A roaring filled her ears. "Forget you, Sheriff."

"Juliet."

The low, commanding tone rippled across her skin. Her gaze lifted involuntarily, a shiver wandering down her spine. She blinked twice. Who was this man, and where was the easygoing sheriff everybody thought they knew?

"Now." He leaned even closer, his minty breath brushing her nose.

She wanted to refuse his demand. Maybe kick him in the shin. But that wasn't who she was or how she solved problems. So she wiped all expression off her face and graced him with a kind smile. "I apologize, Sheriff Lodge. I've been a bit out of sorts today, although I'm feeling better now. But I'm cold. Let's go inside and join the others."

His upper lip quirked. "I have a confession, Juliet. When you try to blow me off with that high-society tone, all I want to do is turn you over my knee and spank you to orgasm."

She gasped, and her eyes widened.

He leaned even closer. "Want me to show you?"

"No." The word emerged strangled, while a fluttering heat wandered down her torso. The man would. He'd actually show her right there outside the lodge. "No."

"Hmmm. Then now's your chance to tell me what's going on." He brushed a stray strand of hair off her forehead.

She jumped. "Um. I don't like lying to your family."

"We're not."

"Yes, we are. You just kissed me, and we're acting like we're really dating." She'd stamp her foot if she were anybody else. Though a lingering panic kept her in place.

"After the other night, Juliet, we are really dating," he said.

She shook her head. Dating people stayed the night together after sex. "No."

His eyes narrowed. "That's not what has you wanting to kick me. I have all day, and I can wait."

The man was impossible. A very unusual temper began to swirl at the base of her neck. "Fine. I just, I mean, I know this is temporary, and I don't want to start acting like it isn't." Darn it. The words slipped out.

He cradled her face, brushing a kiss across her lips. "I'm a jerk."

She crossed her arms. "I don't want to talk about it." Yes. She'd put out her lip and pout if she could. The man drove her crazy.

"Too bad." He grasped her wrists and tugged her arms free, sliding them to trap behind her back at the small of her waist. "We need to discuss this further."

Panic heated through her. No discussion. Plus, pinning her hands was the final straw. She tossed her head, and a satisfying *thunk* echoed when she nailed his chin. Flaring her nostrils, she glared into his dark eyes. "You're messing with the wrong woman here. Back the heck off."

Anger flashed across his face. She'd never seen him mad, and panic had her mouth opening to apologize.

His mouth took hers, shoving the words back down her throat. Then he took. Hard, raw, even angry, he kissed her with a passion that weakened her knees until they trembled. His hands and body kept her trapped, while his mouth destroyed any resistance she might've mustered. With a low sigh, she kissed him back, lost in the electricity generated by a man much more dangerous than she'd realized.

They both breathed heavily when he lifted his head.

She licked her bruised lips, enjoying the flare in his eyes. "I'm sorry I hit your chin."

"I'm sorry I made you feel like this was a short-term, one-night stand by taking you home instead of inviting you to stay the night," he said.

But it was short term. She breathed out. "Okay. We're good now."

"Somehow, I don't think so."

"You are the most stubborn person I've ever met," she muttered.

"I've heard that before." He released her wrists and rubbed a finger across her throbbing mouth. "You mean a lot to me, Juliet. I would've asked you to stay the night the other night but, I, ah, can't sleep with anybody."

She stilled, curiosity taking over. "Oh. Why?" Maybe he snored.

He grimaced. "I have nightmares, and sometimes it takes a little while for me to remember where I am. I can't take the risk of hurting you."

"Nightmares about what?"

His mouth opened and closed. He cleared his throat. "About my time in the service. Things I saw and did."

The man wanted to confide in her. She shouldn't like it so much. "Like PTSD?" She'd heard about the diagnosis from movies on television, but she'd never really understood the concept. Feeling for him, she tucked her hands at his waist.

"Yes," he said evenly.

"Have you ever explained that to somebody you wanted to sleep with?" She ran her palm along his whiskers. His five o'clock shadow made his jaw undeniably sexy.

"I haven't wanted to stay all night with anybody. Until now."

He slid an arm around her shoulders and tugged her toward the lodge. "It isn't an excuse. I haven't found anybody I liked enough to explore the situation with—so it just seemed easier to get out of town. I'm willing to give it a shot now, however."

Hope flared inside her to be quickly quashed. They couldn't have more than right now, because she was out of Maverick as soon as the art show concluded. "Thank you for confiding in me. Now I understand, and I won't push you again."

He exhaled heavily. "Juliet? You're using the high-society tone again."

Quinn held Amy at arm's length through the dance, fighting the urge to step on her foot and break it. What kind of a woman asked a man to dance who clearly had come with a date? For a split second, he'd considered refusing. But the governor had been watching, and Quinn's mama had raised him right, so he'd accepted.

This was the longest song on record.

He glanced around. Someone had decorated the sprawling room with green balloons and purple streamers, lending a party atmosphere to the rough wooden decor. A hand-carved bar made up one wall, a dance floor the other, and tables scattered throughout. A DJ played a collection of country tunes, and a general festiveness filled the air.

His gaze caught on Juliet. Kissing her when she'd arrived hadn't been his plan, but the second he saw her, he'd wanted a taste. The graceful redhead chatted with Colton by the bar. Quinn's heart thumped. Sure, he always figured he'd fall for somebody, get married, and have a family. But his feelings for the woman hit him like a bucking bronc. He figured his ideal mate would be someone suited to the ranch—at least somebody who could ride a horse. Maybe a member of the Kooskia Tribe.

Nothing had prepared him for soft Juliet Montgomery, a woman who lost her temper and still didn't swear at him.

He liked her kindness, her gentleness, her odd, inherent classiness.

Confiding in her had been almost too easy, and his heart felt lighter since he'd trusted her with the truth about his nightmares. Had his taking her home the other night hurt her feelings? He hoped not.

Maybe he was ready to take a chance with her. What if he woke up from a nightmare and hurt her? He'd never forgive himself.

Without question, he wanted Juliet Montgomery in his bed —all night. Maybe it was time to trust not only her but himself.

Though the woman had secrets. He was well trained, and he had excellent instincts. The fact that she didn't trust him hurt. In fact, it damn well pissed him off. He'd tried patience, but soon he'd force her to come clean.

She met his gaze and raised an eyebrow at Amy, who attempted to plaster herself against him. Juliet rolled her eyes.

His instant smile felt good.

Amy tried again to muscle closer. "You smell as good as always, Quinn."

Her perfume choked him. He much preferred Juliet's natural citrus scent. "Thanks."

"Why did we break up, anyway?" Amy asked.

"We didn't exactly date," he said. One foolish night after a fundraiser for Montana forests last year didn't count.

"Why not?" Amy batted thickly mascaraed eyes.

The song ended, and he stepped back. "Thank you for the dance." He made it to Juliet's side just as Colton finished telling a joke. He flashed her a grin. "Juliet, we're dancing."

Juliet pursed her lips. "Loni? Your son is incredibly bossy."

Loni grinned. "He gets bossiness from his daddy and his stepdaddy. I'm an angel."

Colton coughed beer up his nose. "Yeah, Mom. An angel."

"Where are Leila and Tom?" Quinn frowned.

Loni shrugged. "Leila told Tom she hadn't had any Grandpa time lately and was feeling...what was it?"

"Abandoned," Jake said wryly.

"Yeah, abandoned." Loni reached for a glass of wine. "You know Tom—he's a softy. So they planned a day of shopping, an early dinner, and a movie about lost puppies in the city."

Quinn slid an arm around Juliet's shoulders and smiled at Jake. "Your daughter is going to be a dangerous woman someday."

"I hope so." Jake handed Sophie a glass of ginger ale.

The governor and Amy wandered up. He puffed out his chest, and his big belly pushed out the red flannel. "Did you hear about Bennington?"

Quinn slowly turned his head. "What about Bennington?"

"He's withdrawing from the sheriff's race." Amy's eyes lit with glee. "A scandal."

Quinn's gut clenched.

Miles and Shelley Lansing wandered up, no doubt to keep campaigning for Quinn's job. "Did I hear scandal?" Shelley asked.

"Yes." The governor leaned closer to the group, a sly smile on his face, his jowls jiggling as he lowered his tone to a whisper. "Apparently his wife has been growing marijuana in the basement. Five plants. It's still illegal in Montana, you know."

Quinn frowned. "The plants are medicinal, right? I mean, didn't old Mr. Bennington, her father, have cancer?"

The governor shrugged. "I don't care the reason. A candidate can't be breaking the law and growing pot. The news outlets found out about it, and it's over."

It was almost too obvious how the reporters found out. Quinn studied the governor. The question was, how had the governor found out?

Juliet set down her wineglass. "Why would Bennington have to withdraw from the race if his wife was the one breaking the law?"

Amy rolled her eyes. "Really? A candidate must only associate with lawful people, or he has poor judgment. It's the poor judgment, not the pot growing, that will bring down Bennington."

"Oh," Juliet said, reaching to fiddle with her pendant. "How unfortunate."

Colton slid an arm around Loni's shoulders, no doubt not in the mood for gossip. "Mom? Let's dance." He grabbed her and spun her onto the dance floor.

Sophie slipped her arm through Quinn's. "Juliet, do you mind if I dance with my big brother?"

"Go ahead. Just be careful—he likes to lead." Juliet smiled.

"Yes, I do." Quinn directed his statement at the redhead, while leading his sister-in-law onto the dance floor. Juliet blushed, and he chuckled.

The outside door opened, and two men stepped inside. He didn't know them. Both had riding clothes on, but one of them wore boat shoes. He looked closer. The guy with boat shoes had bloodshot eyes and a red nose.

Quinn caught Jake's eye.

CHAPTER 8

*J*uliet enjoyed watching Quinn spin Sophie around on the dance floor. She tightened her hand around the wineglass. Her first and only for the day. A lady never had more than one drink, never leaned against anything, and always smiled in social situations. Her mother had drummed such rules into her head from an early age, and even now, she couldn't help but follow them.

Amy leaned against the bar. "So, you and Quinn, huh?"

Juliet kept the smile in place. "Your boots are lovely, Amy."

Amy glanced down. "Oh, yeah. They're from New York." She glanced up, her eyes sparking. "You know, where you said you visited once in a while."

"Yes. I know where New York is." Juliet ignored the trickle of unease wandering along her shoulders.

"Good, but you're not from the city, right?" Amy's smile flashed too many teeth.

"No." Juliet glanced for an escape from the blonde.

"Politics is a messy business." Amy reached for another drink from the bartender.

Juliet took a sip. "Good thing Quinn isn't in politics. He just wants to be the sheriff to do his job and protect people."

"What will he do if he loses?" Amy gulped her drink.

Juliet's face might go into tremors if she smiled any longer. "Quinn won't lose. He's an excellent lawman."

"Maybe. We'll see." Amy leaned closer. "Our investigators haven't discovered anything about you yet, but they just started looking." With a smirk, she wandered away.

Juliet's throat dried. If her past came out, the news would hurt Quinn. Panicked, she glanced over at him, but he wasn't looking at her.

His focus was on the door.

Two men stood barely inside, their gazes sweeping the area. One wiped his nose on his sleeve. Then he touched the other guy's shoulder and jerked his head toward the bar. The other guy's hands shook, and he sniffed loudly.

Jake grasped her elbow. "Juliet? Please get Sophie and my mom to the restroom." Jake smiled, but the grin didn't come close to reaching his eyes.

An urgency rode his tone and shot butterflies into her stomach. She glanced at Quinn, who gave her an encouraging nod. Numbly, she smiled and glided across the dance floor. Somehow, she gathered both Loni and Sophie on the way.

Sophie leaned in. "What's going on? Quinn sent me to the restroom with you."

"I don't know." Juliet glanced over her shoulder. "Head toward the bathroom, and I'll find out."

"I think you're supposed to come, too," Sophie said.

Yeah, but she might be the problem. While Juliet didn't recognize the guys at the door, that didn't mean they didn't recognize her. "I'll be fine. You're pregnant—get to safety. I'll come get you once I figure out why Quinn is on alert."

They reached the doorway to the restrooms, and Juliet paused to make sure Sophie and Loni headed inside before turning back around. She tried to appear casual, forcing herself to relax against the wall as if waiting for her friend. Her heart thundered, and her mouth went dry. If anybody became hurt because of her, she'd never forgive herself.

The two guys had reached the bar, probably unaware Quinn and his brothers flanked them. Quinn motioned Colton to the side and angled closer to the really twitchy guy.

Juliet frowned. He appeared as if coming down from a bad high.

Quinn hadn't worn his weapon. Why didn't he have a gun? Didn't most off-duty cops carry an off-duty piece? Hopefully, he had a gun tucked in his boot.

The twitchy guy swiveled, big silver gun drawn.

A gasp rippled through the crowd.

Juliet stood up straight. Whatever instincts had told Quinn the newcomers might be dangerous were excellent. She widened her stance. Nobody would get between her and the bathroom door, gun or not.

The guy with the gun pointed the barrel right at Quinn. "Back off."

Quinn held his hands out, stepping away a foot, shifting his body between the man and Juliet. That probably wasn't by chance. "What do you want?"

"Money." His hand shaking, the guy nodded to his friend. "This is a fundraiser, and we want the money."

"Okay," Quinn said, his voice low and soothing. "Barney, give this guy whatever's in the till."

The bartender nodded, his skinny chin wobbling as he hit the cash register and the drawer slid out.

The second guy threw a bag at Barney, and he started filling it.

The first guy laughed, showing yellowed teeth. "This is a fundraiser, man. We want all the money, not only the bar money."

Jake somehow edged closer to the second guy without seeming to move his feet. "The tickets were purchased weeks ago. The only money here in the lodge is at the bar, and you have that."

Quinn nodded. "Take the cash and leave."

The gunman's face turned a mottled red. His hand shook more. "There's no more money?" he yelled.

Jake shook his head. "Nope."

The guy focused on Jake for the briefest of seconds.

Quinn only needed a second. Faster than a whip and just as deadly, he struck out, catching the guy by the wrist and lifting his gun hand. An elbow to the gut, a stomp to the ankle, and the guy went down.

Quinn yanked the gun free.

Jake took care of the second guy with a quick punch to the nose. The guy crashed to the ground, blood spurting.

Colton groaned. "I didn't get to hit anybody."

The guy on the floor lunged up, and Colton nailed him with a sweeping sidekick to the face. The gunman smashed into the bar.

"That's better." Colton grinned, dusting his hands together.

Quinn didn't break a smile. Instead, he removed his cell phone from his pocket and called it in.

Juliet's legs wobbled. She grabbed the wall to steady herself.

Quinn said something that had Jake nodding. Then Quinn's long strides ate up the distance between them. "Juliet? You're pale, sweetheart. Come and sit down."

The kind tone shot tears to her eyes. "How did they get here?" she whispered.

He frowned and turned toward the men. "I don't know. Why?"

"I thought a black SUV followed us to the base of the mountain, but I wasn't sure. Were they in a black SUV?" She shivered. When had the room gotten so cold?

Sirens echoed in the distance. Quinn slid an arm around her shoulders and gently led her to a chair. "Darlin', deep breaths. You're going into shock, and I need you to hold it together."

She nodded.

Two deputies rushed in from outside.

Quinn leaned down to check her face. "I have to give them orders. Are you okay for a few minutes?"

"Yes." She inhaled.

He brushed a kiss on the top of her head and turned to deal with the deputies. Her hands shook. She glanced around at the stunned partygoers. Lansing and his wife cringed in the far corner. Some sheriff he'd turn out to be.

The deputies handcuffed the robbers. Jake hustled toward the back bathroom to fetch his wife and mother.

Time flew by, or maybe she zoned out for a little while. Finally, Quinn dropped to his haunches in front of her. "I had my deputies bring my truck, so I can take you home. Let's go."

She stood and leaned against him, still in a daze. Within minutes she was bundled up in his truck, seat belt secured, a heavy blanket warming her, while Quinn drove down the mountain. Rain peppered the windows. She swallowed. "Do you have to go process those guys—or interrogate them—or whatever?"

"No." Quinn flipped on the windshield wipers. "My deputies can handle the situation. Tonight is my night off, and I'm taking it."

"Oh." She snuggled under the blanket. "How did you know they were going to rob the lodge?"

Quinn glanced in the rear-view mirror. "I didn't know for sure. The first guy shook like he needed a fix, and I trusted my gut."

"They were on drugs?" she asked.

Quinn's jaw visibly tightened. "Yes. Small town problems are no longer a marijuana plant or Peeping Tom. Now we have meth, drug running, and robberies. To get more money for drugs."

"Any chance those guys will get treatment?" she asked.

"I don't know. They pulled a gun on innocent people, so they should be behind bars. For quite some time," he said quietly.

Why did he have to be so black and white? She sighed.

He smiled at her. "I appreciate you trusting Jake and getting Sophie out of the way."

"Of course." Though, in reality, she'd looked at Quinn before moving. "You were really impressive."

"Those guys were morons. Don't be too impressed." His lips pressed together.

But she was. The way he'd put himself in danger, how quickly he'd disarmed the bad guy impressed her. The rainstorm raged around them, yet Quinn remained a solid island in a dangerous storm. "I like you, Quinn," she said quietly.

He flashed her a surprised look. "I like you, too. Feeling a bit vulnerable, sweetheart?"

Man, he could read her. "Yes."

"I won't let anybody hurt you. Ever." The quiet vow emerged deep and guttural.

No, but she'd hurt him. Quinn Lodge wasn't a man you lied to, and she could never undo what she'd done. "I wish we'd met years ago."

He reached over and smoothed the hair off her forehead. "The robbers drove a small compact to the lodge and not a SUV. Why did you think you were being followed? Did something spook you?"

Wow. Talk about foolish. "It's silly. I had a prank call, and then I went outside and my imagination ran away." She picked a loose string on the blanket. "Overactive imagination here."

"What kind of a prank call?" he asked.

"Just a goofy hang-up." Now she'd created problems where none existed.

He leaned forward to peer through the storm. "I can run your phone number, if you want."

She wrinkled her nose. "No, that's okay. It's silly."

"All right, but if it happens again, promise you'll tell me." His jaw firmed.

"I promise." Her gaze dropped to his capable hands on the steering wheel. Broad, rough, those hands could bring a lot of pleasure.

As if he could read her mind, he tangled his fingers with hers. "How would you like to spend the night tonight?"

Her heart leaped. The town bachelor, the sexy sheriff nobody could catch, was offering her intimacy. Pleasure coursed through her to be quickly dashed by icy reality. Every time they were together, she came that much closer to blurting out the truth—and that she'd lied to him. But she couldn't help herself. She wanted this. Wanted him. "You want me to stay the entire night?"

"Yes. The whole night," he said, his voice a low promise.

CHAPTER 9

*J*uliet settled into the overstuffed chair in Quinn's family room, her gaze on the sparking fire, her hand around the stem of a wineglass. Oil paintings depicting the wild Montana landscape covered the walls, and masculine leather furniture decorated the room. "I don't usually drink more than one glass of wine."

Quinn placed another piece of wood on the fire, the muscles in his back shifting nicely. He stood, grabbed his beer, and dropped onto a matching chair. "Why not?"

Her limbs felt heavy. "My mother. She had specific rules about how a lady should act."

"Hmmm." He tipped back his head and swallowed, and the cords in his neck moved with the effort. Sexy and male. "I know from Sophie that your parents have passed on. Was your mother a society-type lady?"

"Yes. Well, she wanted to be." Fond memories lifted Juliet's lips in a smile, and then she grimaced. "My real father drank too much, and I remember a lot of yelling. My mother divorced him and remarried a man with money, and she started climbing the social ladder. Somewhat." Considering Juliet's stepfather lived a life of crime, her mother could climb only so far. But she gave the journey a great shot. "She died of breast cancer four years ago."

"I'm sorry, baby." Quinn's eyes softened in the flickering firelight.

A hard man with soft eyes. Dangerous. Way too dangerous to her heart.

She sipped the cool wine. "How did your father die?"

"A snowmobile accident when I was six and Jake was eight," Quinn said.

Her heart ached for him. "I'm sorry, Quinn."

"Me, too."

"He was full Kooskia, like your mother?" she asked.

Quinn leaned forward on his elbows. "Yes. Is your stepfather still alive?"

"No. He died of liver failure two years ago." While she'd never respected his job, he'd been kind to her, and she missed him. "I'm alone now."

"No, you're not." Quinn leaned back and stretched out his legs. "I promise. You're not alone."

Thunder bellowed outside. The wind whistled angrily above the sound of pelting rain.

Juliet studied the sheriff. The flickering light wandered over his angled face, highlighting his predatory features. Shadows danced along the angles, and suddenly she wanted nothing more than to be his. Even if only for the night. She wanted to belong with the sheriff.

Very gently, she placed her wineglass on the table. She folded the blanket and laid the thick cotton on the chair. Her gaze on the quiet man, she crossed the room and dropped to her knees. His thighs pressed in on her shoulders.

His dark eyes darkened further. "What are you doing?" Low, rough, his voice caressed her skin until a fire sparked inside her.

"Taking you." She unbuckled his belt and pulled the heavy

leather free of his jeans. The buckle clanked when she dropped it to the floor. "Lose the shirt."

Keeping her gaze, he yanked off the shirt. Powerful muscles shifted.

She swallowed. "I adore your chest." Ignoring all decorum, she crawled right up on his lap, her thighs bracketing his. Three round scars dotted his left shoulder, and she leaned over to kiss each one. "What are these?"

"Bullet holes."

She stilled, her heart catching. "Oh." She kissed them again. Then her mouth wandered to a long, diagonal scar across his left pec and rib cage. "And this?"

"Knife." His voice lowered.

"I'm sorry." Deep down, something ached for him. She sat up. Her fingers tapped a jagged scar wrapped around his bicep. "What in the world?"

"Barbed wire when I was a kid." He shrugged. "Rode my bike where I shouldn't have."

She caressed the raised flesh. "You've had a rough life."

"I'm feeling pretty good right now." His eyelids dropped to half-mast. "Is it my turn yet?"

Captured by his tone, she nodded.

"Good." He reached behind her neck and undid her necklaces, placing them on the table. Her earrings were next. "This jewelry is pretty."

"The pieces are Celtic—Irish trinity knots," she whispered, her voice going hoarse.

He slid his hands under her wispy shirt, his palms on her flesh, his knuckles raising the material over her head. "I've never seen a woman more feminine than you."

Hard and fast, the sheriff was sexy. Slow and thoughtful, he was downright devastating.

"Feminine, not fragile." She inhaled his strong scent of male and pine.

He traced her clavicle with calloused fingers. "Fragile, too." His gaze stayed on his fingers as he flicked open her bra and smoothed the straps down her arms.

She blinked, exposed to him.

"You're beautiful, Juliet," he breathed, hands palming her breasts.

"I've never felt like this." He made her feel beautiful.

His dimple flashed. "Every once in a while, you're completely bare. Saying what you feel without holding back." His hands firmed, and he lifted his gaze. "That's how I want you tonight."

Vulnerability slithered right down her spine. "I, ah—"

He rolled her nipples.

Heat flooded to her sex.

With just enough of a bite, he pinched. "I told you how I want you. Understand?"

The dominant tone flashed through her and offered an intriguing sense of safety. One she wanted so badly.

To free herself for one night and take all Quinn could give? The idea should be terrifying. But it would be worth the broken heart and sleepless nights after she left town. She'd always have this to remember.

"I understand. One night. No holding back." She ran her hands up the hard cords of his neck. "That goes for you, too. No holding back."

"I hadn't planned on it." Cupping her head, he lowered his mouth to hers. Firm lips, gentle pressure, so much sweetness in the kiss that tears sprang to her eyes.

Even sweet, a sense of control emanated in his touch. She leaned back and gave in to the need to trace his angular face. "Sometimes, when I've watched you, I wished so badly I was a better sculptor."

He smoothed the skirt up her thighs, his fingers skimming her skin. "When I watched you, I wished for this. For you, in the firelight...becoming mine."

"That's a better wish." She cradled his face and brushed his lips. Her heart jumped even while her mind shut down the fantasy. She couldn't be his. No matter how much she wanted to be. Even if she never broke another law, sometimes a person couldn't negate their past. "I wish more than anything in the world I could be what you want."

"You're exactly what I want." He curved his wandering hands around to cup her rear end. "Someday you're going to tell me what those shadows mean in your eyes, and I'm going to fix whatever is haunting you."

"I wish you could." This whole 'holding nothing back' might get her into trouble. At least she'd have this image to take with her. A strong man in firelight to remember forever. "But tonight, there are no shadows."

"No shadows." He stood suddenly, lifting her with him.

She gasped, her legs tightening around his waist, her hands gripping his shoulders.

"I've got you." The fire in his eyes and low tone of voice held more vow than temporary reassurance. "You're safe."

"You're not safe, Sheriff. Not at all," she murmured.

His dark eyes glittered. "Do tell."

Silky strands tempted her fingers when she threaded them through his hair—and tugged. Just hard enough. "I'm feeling dangerous."

"Juliet," he drawled while carrying her through the room and up the stairs, "I have handcuffs."

She breathed out a combination of heat and humor. "Sounds like a threat."

"Oh no, darlin'." He set her on the bed. "I don't threaten. Ever."

"Really? What was that statement?"

"A promise." He unclasped his jeans and dropped them to the floor. "I'll take a little teasing from you, beautiful. But you cross me? I'll cuff you and make you beg."

Her breath caught low in her throat. She slanted her lips in a small smile. "You have something I'd beg for?"

His smile was anything but small, anything but sweet. "Let's find out." All wolf, he ripped off her skirt. For a quiet moment, he looked his fill. Naked, exposed on his bed, she remained still. The want in his eyes warmed her—gave her a confidence she rarely felt. So she let him look.

With a low hum of appreciation, he slid his hands over her ankles, up her calves, across her thighs. His mouth followed, pausing at her thigh to nip.

Wait a minute. Panic rushed down her throat. This was something she didn't do. She wiggled, partially sitting up to stop him.

He flattened his hand across her stomach. Firm and absolute. His head lifted, and he pinned her with a look.

She swallowed. "No, er, Quinn. I don't ah, do—"

"I'll get the cuffs." His breath brushed her clit.

A strangled gasp hissed out with her breath. He was serious. He'd actually cuff her. Her mind spinning, she lay back down.

He rewarded her with a soft kiss on her mound.

This was way too intimate. She'd lay still, kind of ignore him, and he'd move on to something else. Something she could enjoy. "This really isn't my thing, Qui—"

He licked her. Slow, sure, he licked her. Electric shocks whipped out from his mouth. Static filled her brain.

Those wide shoulders pressed against her inner thighs, forcing her legs open. "You might as well relax, baby. You taste like honeysuckle and spices, and I could do this all night." He spoke right against her flesh, sending vibrations deep into her body. "In fact, I just might."

Her eyelids fluttered. With a deep sigh, she relaxed.

Slowly, one finger entered her. She arched against his mouth, biting her lip to keep from moaning.

A sharp nip to her thigh narrowed her focus. "No holding

back, Juliet." He slid another finger inside her, and crisscrossed them.

A whimper escaped her.

Alternating between licks, nips, even bites, he had her on edge way too quickly. Never quite providing enough pressure to push her over, he kept her at the precipice. Her body stretched tight like a string. Need trembled down her legs. She curled her toes, almost welcoming the cramping pain, just to have something to ground her.

His fingers pumped, his mouth licked, and his deep baritone hummed against her.

The sheriff was playing and truly enjoying the game.

She wanted to swear at him, but every instinct she had warned her not to challenge him. Not right now. He liked her on the edge, and he liked control. So she let him play until she couldn't take any more.

Sweat dotted her brow, her mind fuzzed, and her body gyrated against him. "Quinn, please—"

He lifted his head, even while his fingers continued to torture her. "Please, what, Juliet?"

She tried to concentrate. "You...know."

His dimple flashed. "No. I really don't. Say the words."

The low moan that rumbled from her chest shocked the heck out of her. "Quinn."

"Those aren't the words." He swirled his tongue around her aching clit with just enough pressure to make her sob.

"Stop torturing me," she ground out.

"Want me to stop? Maybe make a late dinner?" He sank his teeth into her other thigh, sure to leave a mark. His mark.

The thought nearly threw her into the orgasm he dangled out of reach. "I may kill you."

The sharp slap to her clit sheeted the room white. "Now, darlin'...threats aren't nice. Do better."

She very well may hate this side of him. "Why are you doing this?"

"You like it."

The fact that her body was on fire, that she was wetter than she'd ever been and was ready to beg? There was something definitely wrong with her, because she apparently did like it. Like him. All of him. "Please let me come."

"With pleasure." Wriggling his finger against a spot inside her that had her legs straightening, he scraped his tongue over her clit with firm pressure.

She exploded like she'd swallowed dynamite. Flashes of nearly painful pleasure shot through her veins, rippling through her. She arched into his mouth, both hands clamping on his head, her body undulating in desperate waves.

Somebody screamed, and yes, it was probably her. She rode out the pulses and murmured his name as she came down. Gasping, she released him and pressed one hand on her chest. Her heart beat rapidly against her palm. "Wow."

"That was nice." He shifted against the bed, his shoulders spreading her legs wider. "Let's try that again."

"No." Her head jerked against the pillow. "No more." She sat up to glare at him. Her body was only partially sated...she needed him inside her and now. "That was great. Wonderful. Now get up here."

His eyelids lifted until his heated gaze met hers.

She stopped moving. Frozen, like prey catching sight of a hunter. "Um."

"Beg me." He said the words calmly.

"No way."

"Exactly." He plunged two fingers inside her.

Her body short-circuited, and she flopped back down. He was going to kill her. Finish her off for all time. But, as his mouth got to work again, she had to admit it wasn't a bad way to go.

Quinn took his time and was thorough. Very thorough. It might have been minutes, perhaps hours. At some point, she was shifting against him, seeking release. Needing to quench the desperate fire he so easily stoked in her. Finally, he moved up her body, taking time to appreciate both breasts.

Then his mouth took hers. Deep, intense, he kissed her like they had forever.

She clasped her ankles across his back, pulling in. His engorged cock lay heavy against the apex of her legs, and she pressed against him, gasping at the exquisite pressure.

He slid inside her, just a bit, and then stopped.

She yanked on his neck, pulling him closer. "Don't stop."

"Don't stop, what?" Sweat sprang out on his forehead. His biceps vibrated as he held still.

"Quinn."

His head dropped, and he sucked her earlobe into his heated mouth. "Tell me what you want."

"You. I want you." She slid against him.

He gripped her hip, holding her in place. "What do you want me to do?"

He was terrible. Truly terrible. "Anything you want. Just do it." She pulled his hair.

His smile flashed dangerous teeth. Pulling her hip up, he shoved inside her with one strong thrust. Her sex squeezed him. Even though she was primed and ready, the shock of his size had her gasping for breath.

Sliding his arms around her thighs, he widened her and began to pound. So strong, so fast, so powerful. He plunged inside her until all she could do was grab onto his defined biceps and feel.

A ball of lava uncoiled inside her.

With a cry of his name, she broke.

CHAPTER 10

*J*uliet snuggled her butt closer into Quinn's groin, playing with the hair on his arm, which lay heavily across her waist. "I like spooning," she murmured sleepily.

He kissed her head.

The storm continued to rage outside, but inside, only contentment reigned.

For now.

"Understand the rules, darlin'?" he rumbled, his body a strong force behind her.

"If you have a nightmare, don't touch you. Don't try to awaken you. I should slide out of the bed and let you wake up on your own," she repeated. Again.

A thick sigh stirred her hair. "I don't like this," he muttered.

"You won't hurt me." She believed the truth in her statement with everything she was. "Believe me. I know."

"I wouldn't mean to hurt you, but you're so small." He shifted as if to slide from the bed.

She grabbed his arm and held tight. "I'm much stronger than you think." Even if he did lash out, she could handle it. Plus, she was only small to him. She had height, and she had strength from lifting more paintings than she could count. "Trust me."

"Hmmm." He relaxed against her.

"I understand how much you like to be in control, and I know this is scary for you." She wiggled a little more. "You're incredibly brave to face this, and I'm honored to be here." It was too bad her demons couldn't be faced down like his. Hers resulted from her own stupidity, and there was nothing she could do but outrun them. "I...care about you, Quinn."

He rolled her over and smoothed hair from her forehead. His dark eyes felt like they were caressing her face. "I care about you, too. This is going somewhere, Juliet."

Her heart shattered. She blinked and opened her mouth to say something. Anything.

He grinned. "No hurry, sweetheart."

Oh, this wasn't good. She couldn't fight them both, and Quinn Lodge was a force of nature, all by himself. How could she explain everything to him? "I know we're good together. But it doesn't change—"

"Change what?" His eyebrows rose.

"You promised. No shadows tonight," she said.

He studied her. The moment drew on, and she could imagine anybody in his interrogation room just giving up and confessing everything. His upper lip tipped up, and he kissed her nose before speaking. "You're not married."

Her eyes widened. "Of course not."

He kissed her mouth this time with a gentle brush of his firm lips. "Well then, anything else I can handle."

If he only knew. In her past, she ran drugs. Kind of. No big deal. No problem, right? Her heart hurt. "Night, Quinn. Sweet dreams." She rolled over, sure she'd never sleep.

Instantly, she fell into dreams of wild storms, raging water, and money falling from the sky that was more of a nightmare than a hope. A definite nightmare.

Morning arrived too soon, and a fully dressed sheriff shook her awake.

She sat up sleepily. "You didn't have a nightmare?"

"Nope." He lifted a shoulder, his gun strapped to his thigh and his badge at his belt. The man looked like he could handle any problem as easy as most people breathed. "We'll have to try again."

She forced a smile. A second chance could not happen. Oddly enough, she'd been the one to have bad dreams, instead of him. All of that worrying for nothing. Of course, she deserved it, and he did not. "Why are you dressed so early?"

"I had a call—need to go to work." He leaned down and kissed her. Slow and deep. Finally, he stood back up. "Take your time. There's coffee on, and I think there are bagels in the pantry. Maybe."

She nodded. "I should get to the gallery. Sophie agreed to have her exhibition moved to an earlier date, and we have a lot to do."

He reached in the night-table drawer and secured a knife to slide into the sheath against his calf, below his jeans. Then he stood, his shoulders wide and strong. The man looked every bit as dangerous as he was rumored to be around town. Tough, protective, and merciless if need be. "Tonight, Juliet. We talk." With a hard look, he turned on his cowboy boot and left the room.

Well, that wasn't good.

※　※　※

THE RAIN DRIZZLED the day into gray. Quinn tipped the brim of his hat to shake off the water, his boots sinking in the soggy weeds. The wind cut through his sheriff's jacket as if it wanted to draw blood. An abandoned barn crumbled behind him, while a dead body lay before him, pale and wan. It had been a while since he'd seen a dead body.

Male, about six feet tall, long, blond hair. Maybe around thirty? "Bullet hole, back of the head," Quinn murmured. "Execution style?"

"Probably." DEA Agent Reese Johnson nodded to the state coroner. "You can take him."

Federal evidence techs bustled around, collecting evidence from grass and dirt.

Reese's phone buzzed, and he looked down to read the screen. "Prints found a match. Leroy Vondoni, recently paroled from Rikers. Shouldn't be out of New York state."

"Rap sheet?" Quinn asked.

"Possession, robbery, intent to sell, assault, attempted murder." Reese tapped his phone. "Nice guy."

Why was Vondoni in Maverick? More importantly— "While I appreciate you calling me in on this, why is the DEA in my county?" Quinn eyed a man he'd trust with his life...in fact, he had at one time. That didn't mean the DEA could set up camp in Montana.

Reese tucked his phone in his back pocket. "We got an anonymous tip the body would be here. An hour later, we were wheels up from LA, and here we are. I called from the plane the first chance I found."

Quinn narrowed his gaze...and waited.

Reese watched the coroner load the body. "I planned to head this way at the end of the week, anyway. Our sources have confirmed there's a large shipment coming down from Canada, and we think Montana will be the entry point."

Irritation washed down Quinn's throat. "Drugs?" What he wouldn't give for a couple of old guys running moonshine.

"Prescription." Reese yanked off his Dodger cap and wiped his forehead. "The new front line. Oxy is more valuable than gold on the streets right now, and I'm hoping there isn't fentanyl thrown in."

"When is the shipment supposed to come through?" Quinn asked.

"Don't know. Gut feeling? Soon. What do you think, Sarge? Your gut has to be humming," Reese said.

His gut was fucking rolling. "Sheriff," Quinn said absently. A dead body in his county was the last thing he needed right now. "Soon is right."

Reese cleared his throat. "Are you going to fight me on jurisdiction?"

"No. I don't have near the resources the feds do. That fingerprint-scanner thing is impressive," Quinn said.

The white scar Reese had earned in Iraq stood out on his forehead. "The machine is yours if we catch these guys. Though why you don't take one of the many job offers you've received from federal law-enforcement agencies, I'll never understand."

"I'm home, and I like it here." Usually. When there weren't dead bodies dumped on forgotten acreage. "The DEA can have this case, but I want in. I want to know everything," Quinn said.

"That means lunch is on you," Reese said.

Quinn gave a short nod, already forming the talking points for his meeting with his deputies later that day. "Tell me this is the first body you've seen in connection with whatever's going on."

"Third." Reese rubbed his chin. "These guys use people and then kill quickly. No witnesses."

Quinn headed for his truck. "How efficient of them. Come into town. I have three deputies I want to bring in on this—we'll keep it to a small task force."

"Fair enough. I'll ride with you. Fill me in on the family. Has Colton graduated yet?" Reese followed, turning to toss his keys at another DEA agent before jumping into the rig.

"He has one more year of graduate school and then wants to

study international finance abroad for a year." Quinn started the engine. "He has already taken over as COO of Freeze-Lodge Investments, and he's been helping to run the financial end of everything for years." Quinn grinned. "We won't give him the salary or the title until he graduates and is home for good, although he doesn't really care, if you ask me. It's the game of the markets that he loves."

"Is he MMA fighting?" Reese asked.

"No. Though he's a tough bastard. He fought for beer money and just a physical challenge, if you ask me. He's the mellowest of us all," Quinn said. Well, until Colton's very long fuse blew. Then everyone got out of the way.

"I caught one of his fights on ESPN late at night. He was brutal." Reese settled into the seat. "With the money you've all made with those investments, why do you work the ranch and sport a gun?"

"What else would I do? Sit around and read ledgers?" Quinn mock shivered.

Reese laughed. "Good enough. So, what's new with you?"

Everything. "Not much."

"Seeing anyone?" Reese asked.

Hell, yes. Quinn lifted a shoulder. "You'll meet her, I'm sure. How about you?"

"Hell, no." Reese shifted his gun away from his hip. "I learned my lesson."

Quinn chuckled. Sometimes romance snuck up and bit a guy on the ass whether he liked it or not. "How does a hoagie from Mrs. Johnson's homemade deli sound?"

"Excellent."

"Good. Now start talking. I need to know how much danger my people are in." Quinn pulled onto the country road.

CHAPTER 11

Several hours after leaving Quinn's place, Juliet struggled to align the small painting depicting horses galloping around the shores of Mineral Lake. She and Sophie had worked all day, and the show would be spectacular. They'd even harassed Colton into helping them mount the larger pieces.

Juliet hadn't heard from Quinn, but rumor had it a cattle rustling had occurred at the north end of the county, so he'd probably been busy.

He wanted to talk. Perhaps she should come clean and tell him the truth. He deserved honesty, even if he ended up arresting her. Maybe she could talk him out of cuffing her. Her laugh lacked humor as it echoed around the room. No way. She couldn't talk him out of an arrest.

She finished fiddling and eyed the main room as a whole. Deep jewel tones splashed across the oil paintings depicting tribal scenes, landscapes, and portraits of fascinating faces. The next room held charcoals, and the final room drawings. Without question, Sophie Lodge had an incredible talent. This showing would put the gallery on the map.

Pride filled Juliet. While she wouldn't be able to bask in the success, she'd accomplished her goals. She'd actually set out and done it. Now, she had to go break Quinn's heart. But he deserved to know the truth. It was time to confess everything.

Grabbing her coat, she locked the front door and hustled out of the building. The rain had stopped, but a tension-filled breeze swirled down the street.

She wandered past storefronts, small restaurants, and a couple of delis before reaching the sheriff's building. Breezing inside the two-story brick building, she nodded at the elderly receptionist, noting the quiet and vacant reception area. "Hi, Mrs. Wilson," she said.

The receptionist pushed her cat's-eye glasses up her nose. "The day's chilly, Juliet. You here to visit the sheriff?"

Juliet nodded.

"Go on back. He's not doing anything," Mrs. Wilson said.

Juliet doubted that. She skirted the counter and headed down the long hallway, passing several offices and cubicles. His office sat in the northern corner and looked out on the street. She paused at the doorway and gathered her courage.

His unique scent of man and leather hit her the second she stepped inside. The fact that he wasn't alone hit her next. She faltered.

"Juliet. Did we have plans?" He rose from behind a scarred wooden desk. Lines of fatigue spread out from his eyes, but they warmed on her.

"Um, no." She glanced at the man rising from the leather guest chair.

Tall, serious, he held himself with coiled strength. Just like Quinn. He held out a hand. "Reese Johnson. I'm an old friend of Quinn's."

"Juliet Montgomery." They shook. She cleared her throat. "Sorry about the interruption. I'll catch up with you later, Quinn." She pivoted to go.

"Juliet." Quinn's quiet baritone stopped her cold. She turned. He grinned and edged around the desk to lift her chin and brush her lips with his. "You're not interrupting. What's going on?"

A man who had no problem touching her, even around an old buddy. Juliet would bet her last penny the old buddy was from the military, too. She forced a smile. "Nothing. Really. I wanted to see if you had dinner plans."

He frowned. "We're probably going to work through dinner. Ah, Reese is from the DEA."

The Drug Enforcement Agency? The words ripped through her with the force of a sledgehammer. "Oh." She turned another smile on the guest, her posture straightening. Was he in town for her? He couldn't be, so she focused back on Quinn. "I suppose you have a lot of work to do."

"Yes." A puzzled light glimmered in his eyes. He grabbed his coat. "Let me walk you out, darlin'."

She stumbled as he maneuvered her through the doorway.

Hustling her out of the station, he grasped her coat lapels. "What's wrong?"

"Everything is lovely." She donned her smoothest smile.

His dark eyes narrowed. "You're the most graceful woman I've ever met, and you just tripped on a smooth floor. Don't get all society-like with me. Something is bothering you, and you'll damn well tell me what it is."

"Nothing is wrong. I mean, I heard you investigated a cattle-rustling call this morning, and then I didn't hear from you, so I was worried." Not true. Not one word was true. She hadn't worried at all until seeing a DEA Agent in his office.

Quinn cocked his head. "You're right—I'm sorry for not calling you today." He tied her scarf more securely. "The call wasn't for cattle rustling. We found a body on the edge of Miller's northern pasture."

She gulped. "A body?"

"Yes. Shot through the head." He leaned down, his gaze serious. "I don't want you going anywhere alone for the time being."

"I won't." She took a deep breath. "Why is the DEA involved?"

"We think the deceased was involved with the prescription drug trade," he said.

So much relief flushed through her, she nearly swayed. Prescriptions had nothing to do with her. Thank goodness her past hadn't caught up with her. Not yet, anyway.

Quinn tangled his fingers through hers and started down the sidewalk.

She pulled away. "What are you doing?"

"Escorting you back to the gallery," he said.

She tried unsuccessfully to free her hand. "That is not necessary. It's barely dinnertime, Quinn. I can walk back by myself."

"No." He tugged her into a sidewalk, his shoulders blocking the wind.

"You're a force of nature, Quinn Lodge," she muttered, stepping over a mud puddle.

He scouted the area on either side of the quiet street. "Thank you."

"I don't believe I gave you a compliment." She sighed. "Is Reese an old military buddy?"

Quinn nodded at a couple of bankers exiting the Maverick Bank for the day. "We served together for five years. He's a good friend."

"You really shouldn't leave him to walk me home. I'm sure you have a lot of work to do," she said.

"He can make phone calls while I'm gone." Quinn slid an arm around her shoulders and tugged her into his heated body. "You're getting all formal again." He glanced down. "What I don't understand is why."

She was saved from having to answer when they turned the corner and reached her gallery.

Quinn stiffened. "Did you leave the front door unlocked?"

The red door stood slightly ajar. "I don't think so." Had she?

He leaned down. Scrape marks slashed from the lock. He pushed her gently toward the road. "Cross the street and go inside the coffee shop. Stay there until I come and get you." Without taking his eyes off the door, he lifted his phone to his ear and called for backup. Then he pulled his gun free of his waistband.

"Now, Juliet." His quiet order held bite this time.

Startled, she rushed across the road. The bell above the door of Kurt's Koffees & Muffins rang when she hustled into the shop. Turning, she pressed close to the window in time to see Quinn nudge the gallery door open with his foot and step inside, sweeping his gun in front of him.

He disappeared from sight.

Every ounce of her control went into keeping still, when all she wanted was to run across the street and make sure he was all right. But she'd distract him when he needed to focus. So she remained at the window, not daring to breathe.

Two police cars screeched to a stop, and a myriad of deputies headed toward the building, guns out.

Thank goodness.

Minutes passed, although it seemed like hours. Finally, Quinn stalked outside.

Relief filled her, and she sagged.

His gaze caught hers, he hurried across the street, and shoved open the door. A thick hand banded around her arm. "Come with me, Juliet."

She nodded, slipping through the doorway. A harsh wind slapped her in the face.

Quinn drew her closer, an arm around her shoulders. "I need you to tell me if anything was taken."

"Okay." She took a deep breath. "Maybe I left the door open?"

"No, sweetheart. You didn't leave the door open." He maneuvered her inside. "Somebody picked the lock."

Dread filled her lungs. "Do you think it was the guys from last year?" Several businesses had been burglarized the previous year by a group of kids from Billings looking for fast cash.

"No. We caught them. Plus, they did the standard smash and grab—broke open the door and grabbed what they could within five minutes. This guy picked the lock carefully. I checked through the gallery, as well as upstairs in your apartment, and didn't discover anything damaged or missing. But you need to check."

The air felt different. Cold and out of sync.

"My laptop is gone." She'd left the HP on the desk by the front door before heading to the sheriff's office. Her heart beating against her ribs, she rushed through the gallery, her gaze on the walls. Sophie's paintings stood bright, dark, and dreamy as silent sentinels to the invasion. But they were safe. No art had been touched or taken.

Thank goodness. Juliet's breath whooshed out. Shaking her hands to release the tension, she followed the sheriff upstairs to her apartment, which appeared untouched. Finally, they ended up in her bright, cheerful kitchen, and she flopped at the table. "I guess they only took the laptop."

Quinn frowned, scribbling in a notebook. "I find that odd."

"That someone would take a laptop? It sounds like a smash and grab like last time." She smoothed out the flowered tablecloth.

He stopped writing. "I'm not sure. Something's bothering me about this. Why pick the lock and leave the door open so you knew? It's like somebody wanted to scare you."

"The entire situation bothers me." She sighed. It seemed doubtful her past had finally found her, but she needed to come clean, anyway. She opened her mouth to spill all, when Reese charged into the room.

He removed his baseball cap. "We have another body."

Juliet's mouth snapped shut. She refused to tell all in front of the DEA agent.

"Over on the south side of the county." Reese glanced at his smartphone. "I have techs on the way. You coming, Quinn?"

Quinn nodded and then grimaced as his cell phone buzzed. He yanked it to his ear. "What?" After listening, he closed his eyes and blew out air. "Is Colton with her? Okay. I'll be there as soon as I can." He hung up and opened his eyes to focus on Juliet. "Rich Jacoby passed away. The ambulance is taking him to the morgue."

"Is Colton with Melanie?" Juliet stood, her eyes widening. Melanie Jacoby and her grandfather were incredibly close and the only living relative either had. Now poor Melanie was all alone.

"Yes. She called him after calling for an ambulance. I guess Rich was unconscious in the barn, and then he died. Colt will help with the funeral arrangements, I'm sure." Quinn grasped Juliet's elbow to escort her to the door. "I'm having a deputy take you to my place. Stay inside until I get home."

She tugged her arm free. Almost. "No. The showing is tomorrow night, and I have work to do."

Quinn's unbreakable grip tightened. "You can finish up tomorrow. For now, I need you safe until I deal with death."

Well, since he put it like that. Juliet fetched two notebooks off the counter. She could confirm details via phone from the sheriff's home office. "Okay."

Lines cut harsh grooves into the side of his mouth. "When I get home, we're going to talk."

Gulping, she nodded. It was time to tell him everything.

CHAPTER 12

Quinn finished with the scene and left Reese to handle his techs. Another dead body, this guy also tied to the drug trade, according to Reese.

The drug trade in Maverick Montana? No way. Quinn would figure out a way to keep the citizens safe. At the moment, he concentrated his gaze on the watery road outside his truck. The rain had increased in intensity, and his vehicle nearly hydroplaned through Miller's Crossing. The deputies had better hurry up and place those warning signs before somebody got hurt. Night was about to fall, and visibility sucked.

His mind spun, and his gut ached. Who would break into Juliet's gallery and steal the laptop? More specifically, who would want her to feel vulnerable?

His radio buzzed. "Sheriff? There's a report of a fight tonight at the high school," Mrs. Wilson said.

He sighed and pressed the button. "I'm on my way."

Five minutes and several lightning strikes later, he pulled the truck into the high school parking lot. Teenagers milled around, forming a circle. He hit his patrol lights. They scattered like scared rabbits through the rain.

Biting back a laugh, he jumped out and grabbed the closest rabbit by the collar. "Mr. Benson. Who's fighting tonight?"

Billy's eyes widened, and he gulped several times. "I, ah, don't know."

Quinn did. His gaze caught on the two young men by the bleachers. The juniors stood, guilt on their faces, hands clenched. Pride filled Quinn that they hadn't fled. "Donny and Luke?" He released Benson with a small shove toward the kid's Subaru.

Donny nodded his buzz-cut head, and freckles popped out on his pale face. Luke shrugged and shuffled his feet.

Quinn lowered his voice to his best "don't-fuck-with-me" tone. "Get in the truck. Now."

The boys almost ran each other over to get in the truck.

Quinn eyed the rest of the group. "Everyone else, go home before this storm strengthens." Pivoting on his cowboy boot, he jumped back into the truck and turned off the patrol lights.

Donny stretched his hands toward the heater. "Are you arresting us, Sheriff?"

Luke cleared his throat. "Um, for what? I mean, we were just standing there. Right?"

Quinn maneuvered the truck onto the road. "You planned to fight."

"Is planning illegal?" Donny asked, hunching his shoulders.

"Could be." Quinn cut him a look. "I'm sure I could find something to book you on."

Luke glanced at Donny. "Your mom is gonna be pissed."

"No shi—kidding." Donny groaned. "My mom is pregnant—very—and on edge."

Luke snorted. "That's an understatement."

"Shut up." Donny elbowed him without much heat. "She's kind of old to be pregnant."

Quinn coughed. "Jesus, Don. She's only thirty-five. That's not old, and your parents started early with you." High school early, actually. But they'd stuck together, and they'd made it.

"Yeah. Old." Donny shook his head.

Quinn took the turn out of town.

"You gonna shoot us and leave us outside of town, sheriff?" Luke asked with a grin.

"I might. You're being such morons, I'd probably be doing your parents a favor." Quinn shook his head.

The tension in the truck abated as the kids realized they weren't headed for the sheriff's station.

"Before I give you hell about planning a fight in my town, especially during a spring storm, why don't you tell me what the fight was about?" Then he'd decide what to do with them. He wasn't finished with them yet.

The boys both shrugged.

"Tell me, or we're heading for booking." Good thing he played poker regularly.

Donny grimaced. "Sierra Zimmerman."

Figured. "You two are fighting over a girl?"

"Yeah," Luke said.

Quinn increased the speed of the windshield wipers. "Sierra is a great girl. Smart as heck and just as pretty. But you two have been best friends since diapers." He'd caught them once stealing apples from McLeary's farm; they'd eaten so much they'd puked as he'd taken them home.

The boys shuffled restlessly.

Quinn sighed. "All right. Here's the deal. If you like a woman, you fight for her. With everything you are."

Two surprised faces turned their full attention on him.

"However, you don't fight each other. You don't fight your best friend. Show some class, show the girl you're a solid guy who will protect her, and give it all you have. With class, strength, and dignity."

Luke scrunched up his face. "That's confusing."

Quinn barked out a laugh. "Welcome to romance. If you two fight over Sierra and one of you gets hurt or embarrassed, then she's hurt and embarrassed. Do you want that?"

"No," they both said instantly.

"Exactly," Quinn said.

Don frowned. "You're a big war hero who carries a gun. Chicks love you."

To be young again. "Have you seen me use my gun?" Quinn asked.

"No," Luke said.

"Exactly. I have a gun, I have training, and I'll use it if I have to. But I certainly wouldn't use it against my friend." Quinn turned into the Maverick subdivision. "If anyone ever comes after your family or your woman, you go after them with absolutely no mercy." He was probably going to get his butt kicked by their mothers for giving such advice, but he'd always been honest with the kids and given them his best. "Other than that, you fight fair and don't scare your girl. Ever."

"Fighting scares girls." Don nodded sagely.

Quinn shrugged. "Frankly, I'm not sure if it scares them, but fighting ticks them off. For the most part, they're a lot smarter than we are."

"That's for sure," Luke muttered.

"So, what are you going to do with us?" Don asked, his gaze on the lightning zigging across the sky. "We know you have something in mind." Luke nodded next to him.

Now he'd become predictable? "Tomorrow you're both offering to clean up leaves and debris for Mrs. Rush and her neighbor, Mr. Pearson, after this storm blows over."

"Pearson's making moonshine again," Luke said.

Quinn shook his head. "We dismantled his still. If he starts walking around naked again, I expect one of you to give me a call."

"He likes being naked," Donny said. "I mean, he's not crazy

or anything. He just said that at his age, the sun feels good on his wrinkles."

"Man, does he have a lot of wrinkles," Luke chortled.

"He's over ninety." Quinn snorted. "So, do you two have any questions for me now that we've talked?"

Donny settled against the seat. "Are you going to marry the art lady?"

"She's pretty," Luke said.

That was not the type of question Quinn had invited. He sighed. "She is pretty, and I just started dating her." He pulled his truck into Luke's driveway. "Marriage is a long way off for me, kids."

Donny glanced at Luke. "As men, we're stupid."

"Morons." Luke leaped out. "Want to come in and play Xbox?"

Donny glanced at Quinn, who nodded. "Sure. I just gotta call my mom. Thanks, Sheriff."

"Make sure you explain everything to your parents, because I will be talking to them." Quinn forced a stern frown. "I'm sure I don't need to tell you what happens if you two decide to fight again."

"Nope," Donny said while Luke shook his head vigorously.

"Good." Quinn waited until they'd hurried inside before pulling out of the driveway. He grabbed his radio. "The high school is all clear, Mrs. Wilson."

"Who was fighting, Sheriff?" she asked, her voice high with curiosity.

"Donny Wilcox and Luke Merryweather were thinking about dusting it up, but they changed their minds. They both like Sierra Zimmerman." He gave her the full story, knowing it'd be all over town the next day anyway.

Mrs. Wilson chuckled. "Sierra is dating the Silvia boy. I saw them at the movies last night." She clicked off.

That figured.

He maneuvered the truck through the storm, his shoulders relaxing when he arrived back in town. After a quick stop at his office, he wanted to get home to Juliet. It was time he followed his own advice and fought for the woman—even if he had to fight with her to get to the truth.

His radio buzzed. Shaking his head, he lifted it. "Yes?"

Mrs. Wilson cleared her throat. "Shelley at Babe's Bar called and asked for you to drop by."

"Me? Why?" He hit his blinker to turn.

"Well, apparently Hawk and Adam are getting into it." Mrs. Wilson sniffed. "Though I doubt it. Hawk just got back in town, and he and Adam have been buddies for years."

"Thank you, Mrs. Wilson. I'll report in as soon as I figure out what's going on." Quinn scowled. He was finished giving speeches about friendship for the night. If Hawk and Adam were being assholes, he'd throw them both in cells until morning.

He double-parked in front of the bar. The scents of tequila, perfume, and sawdust pummeled him as he walked inside. Country music played over the speakers, although the band dais remained empty. Good. Last thing he wanted to deal with was watching his baby sister sing in a bar, while she was home for spring break. Although the girl could sing.

Hawk and Adam stood over by a pool table, beer bottles in hand. Well, no one had thrown a punch yet. Quinn made his way to the back, his gaze on his friends.

"What's going on, gentlemen?" he asked.

Hawk gave him a look. "Nothing."

Hawk owned the ranch to the south of Quinn's and had been Colton's best friend since birth. Half Kooskia, he had dark hair, green eyes, and Native features. Quinn considered him another younger brother and was tempted to smack him just like he would've Colton.

Adam cleared his throat. "Just a little disagreement about my band, Sheriff." He was Colton and Hawk's age. After graduating from college with a business degree, he'd bought the bar in town. He also played in the band and was a fairly decent guitarist.

Quinn shoved impatience down. "Tell me you're not fighting over a girl."

Adam coughed. Hawk stilled.

"You have got to be kidding me." Quinn shoved his hands in his pocket to keep from slamming their heads together. "Tell me you're not fighting over my sister."

"Not like you mean." Hawk took a deep swallow of his beer.

"Explain before I kick your ass, Hawk," Quinn said. So much for niceties.

The outside door opened, and Colton shoved inside. Surprise lifted his eyebrows as he hustled toward them. "What's going on?"

Hawk groaned, while Adam grinned.

Quinn settled his stance. "Somebody was about to explain that to me."

Adam's eyes filled with amusement. "Hawk objects to Dawn singing in the band when she's home during weekends."

Colton nodded his head toward the waitress. "We all object." He smiled when she brought him a longneck. "Not that we don't like your bar or your band, Adam. But Dawn is too young to sing in a bar. Besides, she should be staying at college and having fun each weekend instead of driving home."

"She's legal to drink," Adam said. "I think she's old enough to make up her own mind."

Quinn was more interested in why Hawk felt the need to object on Dawn's behalf. He eyed his old friend, who met his stare evenly and without blinking. "How long you in town, Hawk?" Quinn asked.

"Just a week," Hawk said.

Quinn rubbed his chin. "While you're here, let's all meet up to secure the fences on both our properties before the next storm hits." That way, he and Hawk could have a little discussion.

Hawk's full lip quirked. "I look forward to it, Sheriff."

Yep. Quinn was going to have to smack him a good one.

"Sheriff?" the bartender bellowed. "Mrs. Wilson is on the phone. She said you left your radio and phone in the truck."

Quinn took a deep breath and focused on the bar. "And?"

"There's been a wreck out on the interstate, and they need more spotlights," the bartender said.

"This night is never going to end." Giving anyone within his vicinity a hard look, the sheriff turned on his heel and headed toward the door and his next disaster.

CHAPTER 13

*J*uliet glanced at the dark storm outside and hung up the phone. The caterer would be early the next day to set up, and he'd assured her everything would go smoothly. More than anything, she needed the show to go perfectly. Sophie deserved astounding success.

Wiggling her feet back into an awake state, Juliet surveyed the sheriff's home office. Dark walls lent a masculine atmosphere while the tumbled stone fireplace offered coziness. She could picture him sitting at the solid oak desk, filling out the ranching ledgers. The room even smelled like him. Sexy and strong.

The doorbell rang.

She pushed back from the desk and wandered through the sprawling house to the front door. Glancing in the intricate window set in the middle, she groaned. Then she pulled open the door. "Hi, Joan."

Joan Daniels opened her mouth and closed it quickly. She stood on the porch, casserole dish in hand. A low-cut blouse enhanced impressive breasts. Her tight jeans had to be cutting off oxygen to her feet, which she'd crammed into four-inch heels. "Hi, Juliet. Is Quinn home?"

"No." Ingrained manners forced Juliet to step aside. "Would you like to come inside?"

"Sure." Joan drifted by in a rose-scented cloud. She'd piled her blond hair high in a series of tumbling curls to compliment sultry and dark makeup. She sauntered through the hallway and into the kitchen as if she'd been there many times. "I brought dinner for Quinn as a thank-you for rescuing me from a wild cougar the other night." She set the dish on the granite island. "He had to come out late at night."

"I know." Juliet slid her polite smile into place, wondering who'd save the sheriff from the cougar now in his kitchen. "I was here when the call came in."

"Oh." Joan maneuvered around the island to perch on a bar stool. "Well, you're not the first woman to spend time with the sheriff. He's a handsome man."

Had Joan "spent time" with Quinn? Juliet took the dish and placed it in the refrigerator. Hopefully the woman would leave since Quinn wasn't home. Her manners got the better of her. "May I offer you something to drink?"

"Absolutely. He keeps Wallace Brewery beer on the bottom shelf." Too many teeth flashed when Joan smiled. "I'd love one."

Sure enough, several bottles of Wallace Pale Ale sat on the bottom shelf. Juliet grabbed two and handed one to Joan. Twisting off her cap, she shoved the fridge shut with her hip. "Cheers."

Joan removed her cap and lifted her bottle. "Cheers." She tipped back her head and took a healthy swallow. She hummed. "It's so thoughtful of the sheriff to keep these in stock. He likes the Robust Red, you know."

Actually, Juliet hadn't known that. "Really? He always drinks Scotch when we're out."

Joan frowned. "I wonder why he's so formal with you. The

man likes beer." She leaned forward, elbows on the counter, false interest in her eyes. "Maybe he's not comfortable with you."

Juliet took another sip. "I'll have to ask him when he gets home tonight."

Joan's eyes narrowed. "We'll both ask him."

The doorbell rang. Again.

Juliet set her beer on the counter. "Excuse me." She hustled through the hallway to the door. Hopefully Sophie or Jake had decided to drop by and check on her. She opened the door and smiled with every bit of manners she owned. "Hello, Amy. How nice to see you."

Amy Nelson arched an eyebrow. "Where is the sheriff?"

"Out on a call." Juliet stepped to the side, amusement and irritation battling for control inside her. "Would you like to come in? A neighbor and I are having a drink in the kitchen."

"For a moment." Amy swept by Juliet and headed down the hallway. She charged into the kitchen and zeroed in on Joan. "Hi. I'm Amy Nelson."

"Joan Daniels." Joan glanced at Amy's dress. "That is a stunning dress."

Juliet reached for her beer. The dress was stunning. Sparkling red, the material shimmered and hugged Amy's curvy figure perfectly. "I agree."

Amy smiled. "Thank you. We had a fundraiser for my uncle on the north side of the county, and I introduced him before his speech."

Juliet cleared her throat. "Amy's uncle is the governor. He's running for reelection."

"As is Quinn." Amy squinted at Juliet. "I'm here to talk to him about the rest of his campaign. The man needs to get smart and start campaigning."

"Nobody can beat Quinn. I mean, he is our sheriff." Joan finished off her beer.

"True." Juliet gestured toward the bottle. "Would you like another?"

"Sure," Joan said.

Juliet turned toward Amy. "Would you like a beer?"

"No, thank you." Amy eyed the beer bottle like it might explode. "When will Quinn return?"

The doorbell rang. Again.

"Excuse me." Juliet carried her beer down the hallway this time. "You have got to be kidding me," she muttered. What other woman from Quinn's not-so-distant past would be visiting now? She yanked opened the door and stopped short.

Loni Freeze and Leila Lodge stood on the porch, holding hands. Leila jumped up and down, her cute braids captured in yellow ribbons. "Hi, Juliet! Uncle Quinn said you'd be here."

Juliet grinned. "Hi, Leila. Loni. There's a small get-together in the kitchen. Come on in."

"Whoo-hoo," Leila yelped, releasing her grandmother to skip down the hall.

Loni crossed the threshold, her head tilted. Quinn's mother looked lovely in a pale pink sweater beneath a light green puffer jacket. She smoothed back her thick hair. "Quinn sent us to check on you. They've planned Jacoby's funeral for the day after tomorrow. Poor Melanie."

Remembered sadness washed through Juliet. Being alone made the world a darker place. "Melanie has you and your family, Loni. She'll be all right."

Loni slipped an arm around Juliet's waist. "You have us, too. Don't forget that."

Temporarily, it felt nice to belong. "Thank you."

They entered the kitchen as Leila dropped to one knee, her gaze on Amy's sandals. "Are those Manolo Blahniks?"

"No." Amy glanced down at the three-inch heels. "They're Christian Louboutin."

Leila gasped, her eyes widening. "They're so pretty." She stood and ran to her grandmother. "I love shoes."

Loni ran a hand down Leila's dark hair. "I know, sweetie. I do, too." She glanced around the kitchen, a small smile playing on her face. "Well, this is nice, isn't it?"

"Very." Joan took a healthy swallow of her beer, her disgruntled gaze wandering again to Amy's dress.

Juliet sipped more of her beer. The only thing missing from the party was—

The door to the garage opened, and Quinn Lodge stepped inside. He stopped, his gaze on the gathering of women. A laugh bubbled up in Juliet, but she quashed it. If a "holy shit" expression existed, Quinn was wearing it.

Leila leaped for him. He caught her easily against his chest and smacked a kiss on her forehead. "Hi, Uncle Quinn. Juliet's having a party."

Loni bustled forward and pecked him on the cheek. "We stopped by to keep Juliet company, and turns out she had some visitors. Isn't this wonderful?"

He settled his hand on the butt of his gun in a natural pose. "Ah, yes. Very nice. I, ah, dropped by to grab the spotlight I left in my garage. There's a wreck on the interstate." He set Leila down, his gaze on Juliet. "I might be late."

She nodded, her face heating. Maybe the blush resulted from Loni's delighted grin. Maybe it resulted from the heat in Quinn's gaze. Or maybe it resulted from the glares from the other two women in the room.

Quinn had already shut the door behind himself and escaped to the garage before she regained her voice.

≈ ≈ ≈

JULIET AWOKE from a deep sleep to glance at Quinn's bedside clock. Three in the morning. Something shuffled at the bathroom doorway, and Quinn strode into the room with that male grace she had begun to recognize.

She sat up and clicked on the lamp. "I'm awake."

Wet hair curled around his ears, and he'd tied a towel around his masculine hips. Lines of exhaustion cut into the sides of his mouth, and dark stubble covered his chin. "Sorry if I woke you."

"I didn't even hear the shower." She shoved curls out of her face. "You okay?"

"Fine." He dropped the towel and slipped under the covers, reaching over his shoulder to turn off the lamp.

Instant heat radiated toward her. Should she go back to sleep? Perhaps give him some space?

He made up her mind for her by rolling onto his back and tugging her on top of him. Gentle hands smoothed the hair away from her face. "The wreck was a bad one, but the ambulance arrived in time. I think everyone might be all right."

"Good." She settled more comfortably against his hard body. Soft moonlight filtered in through the shades, and his eyes blazed through the dim. "You were gone a long time."

"Just a couple of hours. After clearing the scene, I had two DV calls to take. I hate those." His hand wandered down her back and cupped her butt.

Heat spiraled through her abdomen. "That means domestic violence, right?"

"Yep. Worst calls ever. I arrested several people tonight— both men and women." He caressed her rear. "Let's talk about something else. How long did your party last?"

A grin tickled her cheeks. "You mean the get-together of women who want Quinn Lodge? Everyone left after you made your appearance."

He snorted. "Funny."

"Not really." She wiggled against his groin just enough to cause his eyes to flare. "This is an awkward question, but I feel the need to ask it. Are you, um, seeing either Joan or Amy?"

"No." He tugged her T-shirt over her head, leaving her in flimsy panties. "I have never dated Joan but did have one unfortunate night with Amy about a year ago after a fundraiser. We all make mistakes."

Jealousy zinged in a weird electric arc into her heart. "She still likes you."

"I like *you*." His voice deepened to a dark tone that wandered right through her skin and warmed her. Everywhere.

"I like you, too." She pressed a gentle kiss against his nose and then looked closer. "Is that a bruise on your chin?"

"Probably." His hands flattened on her butt, pressing her onto his rapidly hardening cock. Even his thighs felt powerful and strong against her. "One of the guys didn't want to be cuffed. We, ah, scuffled."

She took a deep breath, not really having considered the danger he faced every day. "Are you hurt anywhere else?"

"You'll have to discover that for yourself, darlin'." He grinned. "Why don't you start with my mouth?"

"Why don't I," she murmured, brushing his lips with hers.

His mouth captured hers. Deep, strong, he commanded the kiss like he did everything else in his life. Liquid fire rippled through her. Wetness coated her thighs. Her lips trembled and parted for him. He angled his head, deepening the kiss.

A click resounded inside her head. Fire and home. She found her home.

At the frightening thought, she lifted her head. Her breath panted out. Tingles erupted on her lips.

"I wasn't quite done kissing you, Juliet," he rumbled, his dark gaze on her mouth.

"What makes you think you're always in charge?" She slid her knees up to straddle him.

He grinned and slipped his fingers in the waistband of her panties. "If I were in charge, you wouldn't still be wearing these." A quick tug, and he yanked them off.

She settled back into place and lifted an eyebrow. "I'm no longer wearing those."

"I guess I am in charge." He flipped them over and began easing inside her, going slow but not pausing, until he thrust the final inch inside her with one strong push.

With the shock of his entry, she cried out, her body arching into his. Mini-explosions rocketed through her sex. Flashes of light erupted behind her closed eyes. Need cut into her with sharp, demanding blades.

She tangled her hands in his hair, rearing up to kiss him. Hard.

He returned the kiss, his movements slow and drugging. Sexy and deep, he kissed her, consuming all her fear and uncertainty. She relaxed into the safe cocoon created by Quinn Lodge, melted into him with a sense of trust she'd never shared with another person.

His body impaling hers, his mouth destroying hers, he stripped her of any lingering defenses.

Finally, he lifted his head. "You are the most perfect creature I could've ever imagined."

She swallowed, her eyes widening, her heart softening. "Quinn—"

"Shh." He kissed her again, pulling almost out and then sliding back home. "Just feel."

So she did. She slid her hands down to his shoulders. Muscles bunched against her palms as his mouth wandered along her jawline and down her neck.

He pushed hard into her, his pelvis slanting against her clit. Heat zipped up to her breasts, pebbling her nipples. His chest brushed the sensitive buds as he increased his speed, pounding into her until the headboard banged the wall.

Her thighs clasped his, and she tilted up to take more of him. To take all of him.

He thrust harder, his fingers digging into her hip. A ball of fire slowly uncoiled inside her. Then, with a flash of lightning, it detonated into a series of explosions that arched her back. She cried out his name, her nails digging into his skin. Wave upon wave of electric pleasure pumped through her until finally, she went limp.

With a murmur of her name, he ground against her and came.

After several deep breaths, he dropped his forehead to hers. The friendly intimacy slid contentment into her smile. She patted his shoulder. "Sorry about the fingernails."

"I'll wear your marks any day." He withdrew, smiling at her brief whine of protest. Rolling to his side, he spooned her in safety and warmth. "I like having you here, Juliet."

"I like being here." She rubbed his arm. "I'm sorry you had a rough night."

"The night just got a lot better…and drop the society tone. I'm not too tired to spank you." Lazy amusement colored his voice, yet an edge always lived within Quinn.

She swallowed. "That's how I speak."

"Only when you're uncomfortable or trying to control a situation." He tightened his hold. "Before I forget, I was hoping you and Sophie would take Anabella Rush out this weekend. Maybe to a dinner and movie or something like that. My mom agreed to babysit her kids."

Juliet snuggled into the pillow. "Sure. I've met Anabella quite a few times and really like her. Why are you her social organizer?"

"I think the woman needs a night out. Her husband is still overseas, and she needs a break."

The tough, gun-toting sheriff was a softy. "I'd be happy to help." A sudden vision of what life could be like if she stayed with Quinn filled Juliet's mind. She'd be called upon to help with the community, to be a part of so many lives. The sharp desire to be included in such a way stunned her.

"Thanks." He pressed a kiss to the back of her head, his voice slurring with exhaustion. "I'm excited for your showing tomorrow night. You're my date, right?"

Her smile heated her cheeks. "Yes. I'm your date."

"Excellent."

Time to tell him everything.

Quinn began snoring in her ear. Poor guy was exhausted. Well, she'd take the reprieve and tell him all in the morning. Yes, she was a coward and was just fine with that.

She closed her eyes, but her mind kept wandering to the showing. Had she gotten everything ready? What if she'd forgotten something? And where the heck was her laptop? While she'd backed everything up, having her gallery invaded gave her the creeps. Was her past catching up with her?

Finally, she dropped into sleep.

She'd slept for a while before something startled her awake. Her heart smacked against her ribs. She gazed around the unfamiliar room.

A low noise jerked her head up. She slowly turned and scooted up in the bed.

Quinn lay on his side, sweat dotting his upper back. The bedcovers had been shoved to his waist. A tortured groan roiled from his gut.

She forgot his instructions and reached out to place a cool hand on his shoulders.

He moved faster than she could've imagined, rolling over, forcing her down, and pinning her with his body. One broad hand wrapped around her throat. His heart beat hard enough she could feel it through her chest.

"Quinn," she whispered, her trembling hands caressing his chest. "Quinn? It's me, Juliet. Wake up, baby."

His eyes shot open. They weren't focused. His hold tightened.

"Quinn, wake up." She put more force into her whisper. "Wake up, now."

Awareness filtered into his dark eyes, followed quickly by horror. He moved his hand. "Jesus, Juliet. I'm sorry." He made to roll off her.

She shot her legs around his waist and her hands onto his shoulders. "Don't move away."

He closed his eyes and his body vibrated. "Let go of me."

"No." She caressed his chest. "I'm okay. You're fine. You had a nightmare, and you didn't hurt me." She rubbed his whiskers. "Open your eyes."

He did, and the regret in them broke her heart. So she smiled. "I'm fine. You move like an old, slow mare."

An unwilling smile lifted his lip. "I'm neither old nor slow."

His grin relaxed her shoulders. "Unfortunately, you were so slow, I was afraid I'd hurt you, Sheriff. We might need to get you a personal trainer."

He snorted. "A trainer?"

"Don't worry. I took a karate class years ago. I'll protect us," she said.

He lowered himself onto his elbows. "Are you sure I didn't hurt you?"

"Nope. Not at all." She could help him through this—she really could. "I promise."

"Did I scare you?" He lost his smile.

"No." She kept hers in place. "Honest. I knew you'd never hurt me—and you didn't."

Uncertainty had him pausing. "All right." His phone buzzed from the table. He grabbed and pressed it to his ear. "Lodge." He sighed. "I'll be right there." Hanging up, he dropped a kiss on her mouth. "Home invasion on the south side of the county. Gotta go, darlin'." He kissed her deeper until all her bones turned to mush. "I'm looking forward to our date tonight and your amazing gallery opening."

"Me too," she said.

He sat up, his back to her. "Juliet? This, um, means a lot. That you're here and willing to work on this. That you trust me."

The words slammed her in the stomach. She trusted him not to hurt her, but she hadn't trusted him to still care about her once he knew the truth. "I do trust you—and I, ah, have a lot to tell you."

He looked over his shoulder. "Now?"

"No. You have to go, and I need to finish getting ready for the show. Tonight, after the show, I'd like to tell you about my crazy family and the trouble they've gotten me in." She had no choice but to be honest with him. He deserved the truth.

He smiled and somehow, the world brightened. "I look forward to it."

Juliet forced an answering smile. "That makes one of us."

CHAPTER 14

*T*he gallery opening and art showing turned out to be a huge success. People still packed the gallery, although the show would end in less than ten minutes. Juliet wound through bodies, her cheeks flushed.

Reaching Sophie's side, she leaned over to whisper, "I've had six offers on *Storm over Maverick.*" The incredible oil appeared to dance with dark thunderclouds and jagged lightning. "You're going to need to meet with your tax guy to plan next year."

Sophie beamed. "How wonderful." She tipped back her head and finished her non-alcoholic apple cider and place the glass to the side. "A reporter from Los Angeles interviewed me. He's doing a piece on Western art and how the modern paintings compare with the early Remington, Gollings, and Seltzer work."

Juliet clapped her hands. "I'm so happy for you."

"I, of course, mentioned the Maverick Gallery at least ten times," Sophie said.

Juliet grabbed a flute of non-alcoholic cider from a bustling waiter and handed the bubbly to the star of the hour. "You're a good friend, Sophie Lodge."

"Ah, Juliet...I'm hoping we end up more than friends." Sophie glanced over to where Quinn and Jake stood near an open window. "That man is in love."

"So am I." Juliet's gaze ran over the sheriff. Even in the dark suit with a crisp white shirt, a sense of wildness surrounded the man. Contained wildness.

The caterer waved Juliet over.

"Excuse me," she murmured to Sophie. Turning on her decadent three-inch heels, she glided around people to the makeshift kitchen. "How are things going, Raul?"

The stooped man tossed a white braid over his shoulder. A former chef from France, Raul had retired to Montana years ago. He had to be in his mid-eighties at the earliest. "Excellent. It's time to cut off the champagne and collect the empty trays."

"You're the boss." Juliet laughed and headed into the chaos of the empty kitchen.

"Now that's a laugh I've missed." A low voice echoed from around the corner.

Fear made Juliet's ears ring. "Freddy," she said.

"JJ." Her stepbrother came into the room, his smirk baring sharp incisors.

"Darn it, Fred. How did you find me?" Her hands trembled.

He rubbed his nose. "I may not be as smart as you, but I can figure some stuff out."

"Get out of here, or I'll call the cops." Would her past ever leave her alone? She forced herself to keep from running for the hills.

"The cops? Or Sheriff Snuggle-Bunny?" Freddy asked.

Freddy knew about Quinn. Her knees weakened. "There's nothing snuggly about Quinn Lodge. He'll take you out back and skin you like the weasel you are."

"Don't call names." Freddy flashed the diamond in his incisor. A Third Street hooker once told him diamonds in teeth were cool. His tailored leather jacket, black jeans, and spotless cowboy boots couldn't be more out of place in Maverick, Montana. Of course, he only wore the boots because they gave him a couple extra inches in height.

"You look like *My Cousin Vinny*. Without the charm," Juliet muttered.

"I kinda like that movie, Juliet Jennifer Spazzoli." He snorted. "*Montgomery* suits you better."

Montgomery had been her maternal great-grandmother's maiden name. "Why are you here?"

"What? I can't meet up with family? It's been too long." He shoved an entire canapé in his mouth.

If she screamed, Quinn would come running. "Did you break into the gallery yesterday?"

Freddy lifted a narrow shoulder. "I needed a computer and figured my little sister would lend me one."

"What's the truth, Freddy?" she asked.

"I need help." His beady eyes beseeched her. "For old time's sakes."

The door opened, and Quinn stepped into the kitchen. "Hey? Are there any more of those shrimp deals—" His chin lowered as he took in the situation with one glance. "Who's your friend, Juliet?"

Freddy coughed and leaned forward to extend a hand. "Fredrick Spazzoli from out of town. I, uh, collect Western art and was hoping to acquire a couple of the, you know, the amazing pieces here tonight."

They shook hands, and Freddy winced.

Quinn cut his eyes to Juliet. "Juliet?"

She took a deep breath. "His name is Fredrick Spazzoli, he's my stepbrother, and the last thing he wants to collect is art."

Surprise flashed across Freddy's face, while no expression marred Quinn's. He focused back on Freddy. "And?"

Juliet clasped her hands together, drawing dignity around herself like a wool coat. "He's a criminal who has never been caught. I don't know why he's in town, but since there seems to be DEA activity in the area, my guess is Freddy's up to his old tricks of moving drugs."

Freddy flushed a deep red. "I'd watch yourself, JJ."

Disbelief rippled through her so quickly she swayed. "Did you really think I'd lie to him? For you?" The man had never understood her.

"Why not? You've been lying to him since you got here." Freddy snorted snot up his nose.

"Not for you," she muttered.

Quinn squared his stance. "What exactly are Freddy's old tricks?"

"They run the gamut from illegal betting, extortion, petty theft, grand theft, and most recently, drug running." She lowered her own coffin into the ground by giving the truth, but she couldn't turn back now. "My mother married into the Spazzoli crime family. They operated on a small scale...nothing like the mob people you see on television. But, they operated in criminal circles."

Wounded outrage pursed Freddy's lips. "I think that's slander, little sister. I mean, since you have absolutely no proof, and your Cuddles here can't arrest me just on your say-so." He edged closer and stopped when Quinn's shoulders went back. "Besides, if there was a family crime enterprise, you're in the family, now aren't you?"

Quinn turned his focus to her.

She swallowed. "Yes," she whispered. "I'm sorry, Quinn. We moved drugs."

⊲ ⊲ ⊲

QUINN PACED HIS OFFICE, confusion and anger mingling inside him until he wanted to hit something. Juliet was a criminal along with her weak and slimy stepbrother? How was that possible? "I want in on the interviews."

Reese sat in a guest chair, his legs extended, and his new cowboy boots crossed at the ankles on Quinn's desk. "I figured." He read from his phone. "The DEA has suspected Freddy Spazzoli of running drugs since the death of his father a few years ago, but so far, we haven't nailed him."

"Why not?" Quinn dropped into his chair, a thousand pounds weighing him down.

"Anyone able to testify against the guy ends up dead," Reese said,

"The guy seems like a moron to me." No way had the scared dork killed people.

Reese cracked his knuckles. "He *is* a moron. We're fairly certain he's being directed by somebody, but we haven't nailed down who it might be."

"No wonder Juliet escaped." Of course, her statement that she'd run drugs made it entirely possible she'd created a new life to evade the law.

Amusement lit Reese's normally serious gaze. "Speaking of your love, how long are you going to let her stew in the cell?"

"At least she's safe in the cell." Quinn had arrested both Juliet and Freddy the second Juliet had dropped her bombshell, hustling them out the back door and to the station. "Until I arrest her for running drugs. Or until you do." This still wasn't possible—there had to be a logical explanation.

Reese's phone beeped, and he read a message. "There's no record whatsoever on Juliet Spazzoli. Her mother married Dominique Spazzoli when Juliet was ten and changed Juliet's last name at that time."

Quinn frowned. "Spazzoli didn't adopt her?"

"No. Just the name change. Dom Spazzoli owned several

illegal betting operations but didn't run drugs. For a criminal, he was one of the decent guys. I mean, sure, he broke some laws, but he didn't sell drugs to kids."

"Unlike Freddy." And maybe Juliet.

Reese's brow furrowed. "We don't have any proof against Freddy. Even if Juliet provides proof, according to her own statement, she's a coconspirator. We can't arrest Freddy just on her word."

Quinn shoved a hand through his hair. "I'm not using Juliet's statement against her until I talk to her officially." The woman had clammed up the second he'd arrested her, regally lifting her chin. She was the most graceful prisoner he'd ever cuffed and escorted into a jail cell.

Reese shrugged. "We're talking federal law here. Her statement doesn't hurt her any more than it hurts Freddy…unless we get corroborating evidence against one of them. Considering she just confessed, I'd bet my shiny new boots she has evidence we could use against both of them." He leaned forward. "How well do you really know this woman?"

"Apparently not well at all." Quinn was 100 percent in love with a woman he didn't know. How crazy was that? Love or not, if she'd been involved with the drug trade, she wasn't who he thought. "I wish we could tie Freddy to the local murders. Then he'd give up his partner or boss or whoever the guy is."

"The operation is believed to span several states. We're talking federal trafficking here," Reese said.

Dread slammed into Quinn's gut. Juliet would to go jail for life if she'd been involved in the drug trade. "There has to be some mistake."

"There's no mistake," Reese said slowly. "I definitely want Freddy and his partner on the trafficking and murders. Maybe we could talk to the federal prosecutor about some sort of deal with Juliet—if she has proof that hurts Freddy, or if she knows who Freddy is working with and is willing to testify."

Hope commingled with fury inside Quinn, but he kept his face impassive. "I'm sure that will be an option—once we find out the entire truth. So far, I'm not believing Juliet willingly trafficked drugs." He couldn't be that horrible a judge of character, could he?

"Are you thinking with your head or your dick?" Reese asked.

That the question was valid pissed off Quinn more than he would've believed possible. "Don't make me shoot you."

Reese lifted a shoulder. "The DEA has waited long enough, and now I'm going to interview my suspect. You in or out?"

Quinn clenched his hands. "I'll get her." He stomped from the room, taking deep breaths to maintain control. It'd been years since he felt on edge like this, and he needed to hold it together. The long hallway stretched forever until he reached the first cell. Still wearing her sexy black dress with the sparkly silver shoes, Juliet looked like a captured princess in the dismal cell.

A feminine and fragile princess.

Keys jangled against the old lock as he released the bars. "Come on, Juliet."

Her pale face whitened further, but she rose gracefully from the single cot. "Where?"

"Interrogation." Every instinct he owned wanted to reach out and gather her close for a hug. "The DEA wants to interview you about your statement to me."

She nodded, regally lifting her head and gliding past him into the hallway. "Your friend, Reese?"

"Yes." Quinn relocked the door. He'd put Freddy in a cell at the far end of the cell block and had every intention of leaving him there until Reese wanted to talk to him.

She stopped. "Quinn, I—"

"Save your statement for the DEA. I don't want to hear it." Quinn motioned her ahead of him, his gut clenching at how her hands trembled. Didn't she know he'd have to testify about anything she said to him?

"Of course," she said formally. "I apologize."

For the first time in eight years, he hated the fact that he was the sheriff.

CHAPTER 15

*J*uliet shifted on the cold metal chair in the interrogation room. Chilly and intimidating, the room was small with unadorned, dingy, white walls. "I understand my rights as you've read them to me."

Reese nodded from across the scarred wooden table. "All right. Let's get started."

Quinn leaned against the far corner, his massive arms crossed. "No. Not yet."

Reese raised an eyebrow. "Sheriff Lodge, if you're going to be difficult, I'll ask you to leave."

Fire lanced through Quinn's gaze. In the loosened white shirt and black suit, he looked like a panther ready to strike.

Panic lanced Juliet's chest. Two old friends might fight because of her. "I'm ready to get started, and I'll answer anything you ask."

"No, you won't," Quinn ground out.

"Why not?" Reese asked, irritation curling his upper lip.

The door slid open. "I assume it's because my client is waiting for her lawyer." Smooth as silk, Jake Lodge stepped into the room. He'd donned a slate-gray Armani suit and carried a hand-stitched leather briefcase. "Would you gentlemen please excuse us so my client and I can confer?"

Reese slowly turned his head to glare at Quinn. "You called your brother?"

Quinn headed for the door. "She has a right to a lawyer. I figured, why not get the best?" He disappeared into the hallway.

Reese stood and rounded on Jake. "You have ten minutes."

Jake smiled. "I'll take as long as I want, Agent Johnson. Now get out." He slid into Reese's vacated spot.

"Fine. I'll go talk to Freddy now." Reese swore under his breath as he left the room. The door slammed shut.

Jake's face gentled. "How you holding up?"

Tears pricked the back of her eyes. "Not so well. Quinn is mad at me."

"Ah, yes. But we need to be concerned with the drug charges right now, Juliet," Jake said.

"He's really angry with me." Who cared about drugs? She wanted Quinn to look at her like he did yesterday.

Jake coughed into his hand. "I need you to focus here."

"Of course." Relying on years of experience, she drew dignity close. "What do you want to know?"

Jake lifted one dark eyebrow in an expression Quinn often wore. "Everything."

Juliet took a deep breath. "All right, but I'm only telling the story once. Please ask Quinn to come back."

"Sheriff Lodge will be subpoenaed to testify as to anything you say. Let's bring him into this conversation after I figure out our best move," Jake said gently.

Juliet straightened. "I'm going to tell him everything, anyway. You're my lawyer, and you have to follow my wishes."

"Your wishes are going to land you in federal prison." Jake rubbed his scruffy jaw. Apparently he hadn't had time to shave when changing clothes. "It's well after midnight, you're tired, and you might not be thinking clearly. Trust me on this. You don't want Quinn in here quite yet."

"I can't do this twice, and he deserves to hear the full truth." He'd given her his trust, and she owed him. So she had to tell the full truth and not hide behind the law.

Jake shook his head. "You're acting against the advice of your lawyer."

"I know," she whispered.

Jake stood and ripped open the door. "Quinn?"

Quinn appeared immediately. "What?"

"She wants to include you in this meeting." Still shaking his head, Jake retook his seat.

Quinn frowned. "That's crazy."

"I know, but she only wants to tell the story once." Jake grabbed a legal pad from his briefcase to slide onto the table.

Juliet looked at Quinn. "Do your job and listen to my story, Quinn."

His jaw tightened until it had to hurt. "You're putting me in a terrible position."

She sighed. "Let's get this over with."

Anger blazed in his eyes, but he retook his position in the far corner. Of course, he'd followed duty. She'd counted on his sense of honor.

"I lied to you, and I'm sorry." Clearing her throat, she focused her gaze on her hands. "When I turned ten, my mother married Dominique Spazzoli. He was a criminal. Mainly illegal betting operations, but probably some blackmail and extortion. He took me in, gave me a home, and I loved him." She swallowed and glanced at Quinn's expressionless face. "I know he was a criminal, but he was good to me." Not even to get out of a federal drug charge would she say anything bad about Dom. He was the closest thing she had to a father, and he'd loved her, too.

"Did you partake in any illegal activity growing up?" Quinn asked.

Jake jerked his head toward Quinn. "You're invited to listen and not ask questions, Sheriff."

"Bullshit." Quinn's arms uncrossed. "I'm here, and I'm partaking. Deal with it, counselor."

Wonderful. Now the brothers might come to blows. Juliet cleared her throat again. "No. Dom kept me as far away from the criminal activities as possible. He didn't deal with drugs. Freddy entered the drug trade when Dom died."

"You entered with him?" Quinn asked.

A shiver racked her. "Of course not."

"It's too cold in here." Quinn yanked off his suit jacket and dropped the heavy material over her shoulders.

Instant warmth and the scent of male surrounded her. Something inside her stomach softened. "Not on purpose. The Children's Art Clinic of New Jersey hired me to teach a couple of classes a week to kids. I had so much fun teaching those kids how to sculpt." Her hands trembled, so she clasped them together. "The CAC is a nonprofit that exposes underprivileged kids to the arts. The job didn't pay much, but I loved it."

Jake tapped his silver pen on the pad. "The CAC was a drug front?"

"Not at all. Freddy put the drugs in my trunk, I drove from New York to Jersey, and somebody would take the drugs out while I taught classes."

Quinn dropped into the one vacant chair by his brother. "Did you know?"

"No." She allowed her own stupidity to reflect in her voice. "For six months, I ran drugs, and I had no clue."

Quinn shook his head. "The kind of danger you must've been in..."

She nodded. "I'm a moron. How could anybody have no clue they were trafficking drugs across state lines for six months? But really, how often to you look in your trunk if you're not storing stuff?"

Quinn stared at his brother. "If she had no idea, if she had no intent to traffic, there's no crime, right?"

Jake slowly nodded.

Juliet shook her head. "Seriously? I'm Dom Spazzoli's step-daughter and Freddy Spazzoli's stepsister. No way would a federal prosecutor or jury believe I remained unaware of the drug transfer. Period."

"She has a point," Jake said.

"Besides"—she picked at a sequin on her dress, wanting to get it all out there—"I didn't call the cops once I found out. I called Freddy and yelled at him. He had me look at a building across the street that had a camera pointed right at me. I was on camera for six months. Freddy believes in insurance policies."

"Did the cameras ever catch you looking in the trunk?" Jake asked, scribbling on his notepad.

"Not until the day I discovered what was going on," she said quietly. Crap, she really needed to tell the whole story. "So, I got out of town. I mean, I acquired false identification and got out of town."

Jake held up a hand. "I believe what my client means is a friend of hers supplied her with false identification. She neither purchased it, nor has she used it since."

Juliet frowned. "No, I—"

"Good enough," Quinn growled. "We can revisit the false-identification issue later. For now, I want you to tell me every-thing you learned about Freddy's drug business."

The door opened, and Reese pushed a rickety cart holding an older television on top of a DVD player. "Freddy was very cooperative and supplied me with a video that is quite intrigu-ing." He plugged in the electronics and grabbed a rusty remote.

Jake slammed his pen down. "We're in the middle of something."

Reese flashed a dangerous smile. "I understand what you're doing. However, why don't we watch this video? Afterward, I'll leave so you can confer with your client on how she wants to plead this out."

Ice-cold fingers traced Juliet's spine. This was so not going to be good. Her shoulders straightened, and she flashed Quinn an apologetic grimace. "Push play, Agent Johnson."

Reese engaged the television and player before starting the video. Several minutes went by that showed several wrapped white packages put into her trunk in front of her apartment in New York and then taken out of her trunk in New Jersey. The men involved were Freddy's lackeys, but not once did Freddy make an appearance.

Quinn wandered to lean against the far wall.

Jake stretched his neck. "First, there's no proof those are drugs. Second, not once has Juliet been on screen with the trunk open. You've got nothing, Agent."

Reese pressed a button. "Let's fast-forward to the end, shall we?"

Juliet briefly closed her eyes. "Good idea."

The tape scrolled forward until it showed the events of the day that changed her life forever. The camera captured her leaving the art clinic just in time to see a man slam her trunk closed. She stilled, and he ran away. A frown marring her face, she'd hustled forward and opened the trunk.

Cash. Tons of wrapped and stacked cash lined her entire trunk.

The interrogation room went deadly still.

Even with the grainy camera, there was no question that a lot of money sat in her trunk.

She'd whipped out her cell phone and called Freddy, who'd laughed his head off when explaining the cameras. She'd turned to look directly at the camera while still on the phone. Slowly, she'd ended the call, torn her cell phone apart, and left the shattered pieces on the pavement. After slamming the trunk shut, she'd gotten in the car and driven off.

The recording went fuzzy and then black.

Reese turned off the television. "As you can see, counselor, your client drove off with full knowledge her trunk was full of cash. She had enough knowledge of her family to know that it was probably drug money. She neither called the police nor the DEA. What she did do is disappear from town with the money. That's theft at the very least, and more than likely, accessory after the fact on the drug charges."

Juliet opened her mouth, and Jake shook his head. "Don't speak."

She nodded. Her driving away with all of the cash looked horrible for her.

Reese continued, "I think I can get her on trafficking drugs, however. A jury is unlikely to believe the 'I-didn't-know' defense. They rarely do." He slammed the remote down on the table.

Juliet jumped.

Reese leaned in. "I understand why you ran. Stealing so much money from Freddy and his cronies certainly put a hit out on you. I'm going to leave now, and you and your attorney are going to figure out how to turn the money over to the DEA and what type of evidence you can come up with to send your brother to jail. It's your only hope."

"I have no evidence against Freddy." She ignored the warning flashing in Jake's eyes. "Besides, the money is gone. Every last dollar."

Jake motioned Reese to back up. "Okay, we're going to talk in hypotheticals now. Does everyone understand?"

Slowly, both Quinn and Reese nodded.

"Good." Jake peered at her. "Hypothetically, even though you have no knowledge of any money, what would a woman in the situation like the one you just saw on the tape have done with all of that money?"

The moment seemed a bit late for hypotheticals, but what

the heck. Juliet lifted her chin. "Hypothetically? I suppose the woman would've had some fun giving all the money away. Maybe some to the Art Clinic, some to the First Baptist Church on Delaney Street that needed a new roof, some to the Catholic Church around the corner, some to the boys baseball club in southern New York for new backstops. I suppose then the woman would give money to charities and churches as she drove west to safety. Until it was all gone."

Reese staggered back. "All gone?"

Jake chuckled. "I don't suppose the woman would've kept track of where all the money went?"

She plastered on her sweetest smile. "I would assume a woman like that would've kept track. Definitely."

Reese shook his head. "You had start-up money for the gallery."

"That was drug money, and I'd never use it." She clasped her hands together. "If you check my bank records, you'll see I emptied out my savings as I left town. I used my own money to start the gallery." All of her money, in fact. She hadn't used one cent of Freddy's drug cash.

Jake pushed back from the table and stood. "My client and I are leaving."

Reese held up a hand. "Wait a minute."

"No." Jake skirted the table and assisted Juliet up. "She has cooperated fully with you. All you have is a mistaken statement made to her current lover when she was under extreme duress. While the video of her finding something in her trunk is interesting, it has neither been authenticated nor truly examined. We're not even sure that's Juliet, much less money in the trunk. Even if you do somehow prove that was cash, nobody has reported cash being stolen. Therefore, you can't prove whose cash it was. Hypothetically, of course."

Wow. Juliet stumbled along with Jake to the door. He really was an amazing lawyer.

Jake paused. "While I have no doubt you'll be meeting with the federal prosecutor soon, Agent Johnson, you don't have probable cause for an arrest. You know it."

Quinn cleared his throat, looking so big and dangerous he seemed to take up all the space in the room. "She's in danger, Jake. We don't know who's in town with Freddy, and we don't have anything to hold him on."

Juliet tried to catch Quinn's eye, but he kept his focus on his brother. Hurt cut into her heart. In trying to keep him, she'd lost him.

Jake nodded. "She's staying with Sophie and me. We'll keep her safe, and we'll bring her to the Jacoby's funeral tomorrow."

"Good. I'll talk to you later." Just as smooth as that, Quinn Lodge excused her from not only the room but his life.

Juliet's chin rose, and she followed Jake away from interrogation and Quinn Lodge.

CHAPTER 16

*R*ain pattered around the gravesite. Juliet shifted her boots on the wet grass and edged closer to Sophie under the sprawling umbrella. While she wanted to be respectful and keep her focus on the preacher or the coffin being lowered into the ground, her gaze kept straying to Quinn.

He stood next to Melanie as they said good-bye to her grandfather. He'd left his Stetson in the truck, and the rain slid down his angled face unchecked. Sadness darkened his already dark eyes, and his black hair curled at his nape. A calm in the storm, he maneuvered closer to Melanie when she trembled.

Colton flanked Melanie's other side, an arm around her shoulders. The woman's thick, brown hair curled down her back. The rain only added to the wild curl. Her brown eyes glimmered with tears, and, sandwiched between Quinn and Colton, she appeared breakable. She clutched a bouquet of pink roses. Colton whispered something into her ear, and her lips tipped in a small smile. She leaned into him as the coffin came to a rest.

The preacher finished his eulogy, and Sophie tucked her arm

through Juliet's. "I'm glad Colton can be here for Melanie right now."

"Me, too," Juliet said softly. "Though I thought Melanie dated a banker." She'd seen them in town together. The man always wore a three-piece suit but didn't seem to be present today.

"She is, for now. I guess he's at some conference in London. Apparently he's flying home tomorrow." Sophie turned toward the cars. "Let's head to the wake early to make sure everything is set up."

Juliet stumbled in her high-heeled boots. "Actually, do you mind dropping me at home? I think I'll skip the wake."

"Juliet Spazzoli." Sophie tugged her through bodies toward the road. "You are not hiding just because your boyfriend hauled you down to the station for questioning. Grow a pair, girlfriend."

Jake snorted next to her. "I truly wish you'd stop using that expression, Sunshine."

Sophie shrugged. "You grow a pair, too, counselor." Then she yelped as Jake snaked an arm around her waist and lifted, turning her midair to face him.

Juliet grabbed the umbrella handle before a spoke pricked her forehead. She paused as Jake easily held his wife a foot off the ground, determined amusement darkening his eyes. Sophie's eyes widened. Yeah, the Lodge brothers didn't take kindly to challenges.

With a shrug, Juliet left the couple. "I'll meet you at the car."

She picked her way around gravestones and the hilly terrain. As she reached the car, a strong hand banded around her arm. The scents of pine and male surrounded her, and her heart galloped into motion. Slowly, she turned. "Good afternoon, Sheriff Lodge."

He ducked to keep from getting smacked with the umbrella. "I'll give you a ride to Mel's house."

"That's kind of you, but I'm returning to my apartment." She fought a wince at how formal she sounded.

"No, you're not." Quinn took the umbrella and, keeping her head shielded, led her to his truck. "We had to cut Freddy loose, and I'd rather keep an eye on you until I figure out what he's doing."

"While I appreciate your concern, I've been taking care of myself for quite some time." Yet her legs kept moving right alongside his. Might as well poke the bear sooner rather than later. "Let go of my arm, or I'm going to kick you in the knee."

He opened the passenger door and glanced down at her boots. "Those are kind of pointy."

She closed the umbrella. "Yes, they are. I assume they'd do some damage."

"You've already been to the jail once. Do you want another trip for assaulting a police officer?" His head cocked to the side, but no expression filtered across his rugged face.

"Not really. However, if I'm not under arrest, you can't make me get in your truck," she said.

Predictably, he did exactly what she wanted him to do. Both hands grabbed her waist, and he lifted her into the truck. At the one touch, desire flared awake through her entire body. Several deep breaths did nothing but make her abdomen ache more.

She waited until he'd shut the door, crossed in front, and jumped into his seat before speaking, "I knew you were going to do that."

"Darlin', we both knew I was going to do that." He started the ignition. "We obviously need to talk."

Her stomach ached. "You're mad at me," she said.

"Furious." He nodded at a couple of people walking along the road toward the long line of cars. "Put on your seat belt."

Something in her chest splintered. "Does this mean we're over?"

"Right now? I have no clue. I need to deal with making sure

Melanie is all right, making sure Colton doesn't screw up his future, find out why drug dealers are killing people in my county, fight to keep my job, and get your stepbrother out of your life for good." His knuckles turned white on the steering wheel. "You lied to me. There have been times in my life when trust was the only thing I could rely on. I...need time to figure things out."

The splinter in her chest exploded. "When I was eighteen, I fell in love with a guy named Sonny Mitchsi."

Quinn's nostrils flared. "He was a criminal?"

"No. Sonny was a genius—got a full ride to business school," she said.

"All right," Quinn said.

"The second he found out about my family, he dumped me. Said he couldn't be involved with somebody like me—somebody with a family like mine." Remembered hurt slithered down her spine. "I didn't want you to do that."

Quinn grunted. "You didn't give me the chance."

She sighed—he was right. "I didn't ask to get in your truck."

"I know." He glanced in the rearview mirror. "Jake and Sophie needed a moment, and so did you and I."

"Am I going to go to jail?" Juliet asked quietly.

"No. You have the best lawyer in the world, and frankly, you didn't do anything wrong." Quinn pulled the truck onto the main road. "Well, anything illegal. You didn't do anything illegal."

Oh, but lying to him was wrong. Lying to him and then sleeping with him, that is. If they'd remained just acquaintances, the lying probably wouldn't have mattered much. Now it seemed like everything. "I'm sorry, Quinn."

"Me, too." He tossed his black Stetson on the dash. "You didn't trust me, Juliet."

There was the crux of the problem. Everyone leaned on and

trusted Quinn Lodge, yet she was the only person he'd opened up to. No wonder he was so mad.

"I am curious. How long were you planning to stay in town?" he asked.

Chills cascaded down her back. "I planned to leave after the showing."

His firm jaw snapped shut. "I see. Where were you going?"

"I thought I'd go to Utah or Wyoming." Somewhere there were mountains, cowboys, and a community. But no place would have Quinn Lodge. "I'm sorry."

They rode the rest of the way in silence, finally pulling to a stop in front of Melanie's white farmhouse. A porch wrapped around the entire first floor, the planks faded and a few in need of repair.

Quinn frowned through the windshield. "I hadn't noticed Old Man Jacoby needed help. Apparently I should've paid closer attention." He stepped out of the truck and crossed behind it to open Juliet's door.

She allowed him to assist her to the gravel. His hands lingered at her waist, and his eyes darkened.

"Sheriff?" someone called out.

They both turned and a flash went off. Several flashes peppered the air. Scowling, Quinn stepped in front to shield her.

The photographer rushed toward a parked car and sped off.

Juliet pursed her lips. "What was that all about?"

"I don't want to know." Quinn closed her door and took her elbow to escort to the porch.

"But, if that was a reporter, do you think they found out about me?" Oh, no. Any scandal could destroy Quinn's campaign.

"Maybe." He released her. "I'll see you inside." Without another word, he hurried to where his mother emerged from a truck, her hands full of dishes. After pecking Loni on the cheek, he reached for the bundle.

A lonely chill squeezed Juliet's chest. She would've liked having been part of the Lodge-Freeze family. Sighing, she went inside for the wake.

THE MORNING AFTER THE FUNERAL, Juliet poked her head outside the gallery door. "Deputy Baker? Would you like some coffee?"

The young officer shook his head. "No thank you, ma'am." He turned his red head back to survey the quiet street.

"How about you come inside and warm up? You can guard the gallery just as well from inside." She fought guilt—the poor guy had been outside all night, just trying to protect her from her own family.

"Thank you, ma'am, but the sheriff left strict instructions for me to stay right here until my replacement arrived." The kid didn't change his focus.

Sighing, Juliet closed the door. Quinn was punishing her for her decision to return to her apartment and not impose any longer on Sophie and Jake. She punched in numbers on her landline and asked to speak with the sheriff. Mrs. Wilson said she'd take a message, but that the sheriff was out on a call. Juliet decided not to leave a message.

Instead, she hustled to her desk in the corner to balance her books. After the exhibit the other night, she was finally in the black. Thank goodness.

An hour passed.

Then another.

Suddenly, the door blew open. She yelped and jumped. The sheriff stood in the doorway, gun out, his face a concentrated mask. "Juliet?"

She pressed a hand to her chest. "Why is your gun out?"

He frowned and set his gun back in the shoulder holster. "I got a report of screams coming from the gallery."

The young deputy sidled in from the other gallery. "There wasn't anybody in the back entrance, sheriff."

Quinn's gaze narrowed. "You didn't hear any screams?"

"No, sir," the officer said.

"I think it's a hoax," Quinn muttered.

The deputy scratched his chin. "Who called it in?"

"I don't know. It was a call to dispatch. Take point outside, Baker. Phillips will be here in five to relieve you." Quinn waited until the deputy took his leave to focus on Juliet. "I also had a message you called."

She ran her hand along the back of her chair. "I'm refusing police protection. Please keep your deputies off my property."

A veil dropped over his eyes. "You're in danger, now there's a prank call regarding you, and you don't get to refuse police protection."

She glowered. "You're trespassing, Sheriff Lodge. Please leave."

"No." He crossed his arms.

For the love of all that was holy. Stubbornness lived in the man, at home and comfortable. "We broke up." She understood exactly what 'I need time to think' meant. "As such, you no longer need to concern yourself about me. All of the truth is out, and Freddy probably has no interest in me. Especially since Jake explained to him that the money is long gone."

"Regardless of the status of our relationship, you're a citizen in my county. If you're in danger, you get police protection." Quinn leaned against the door. "Deal with it, Juliet."

Anger rippled through her veins. So she plastered on a polite smile and straightened her shoulders. "Well, then, I thank you for your diligence, Sheriff Lodge. The citizens of Maverick are fortunate to have you protecting us."

Temper rippled across his face.

His phone buzzed, but his dark gaze kept her pinned while he answered. "I'll be right there." Turning on his heel, he yanked open the door to reveal a different deputy at guard. "Stay with her and report in hourly." Without looking back, he strode out of sight.

The door drifted closed.

Her phone rang, and she cleared her throat before answering, "Maverick Gallery."

"Hi, Juliet. This is Mrs. Hudson, from down the street?" an elderly voice chirped.

"Hi, Mrs. Hudson." Juliet took another deep breath. The sweet widow lived in a small cottage a block down the street, and Juliet often dropped off groceries or goodies for the woman.

"What can I help you with?"

"Oh, Juliet. I dropped my favorite earrings—you know the ones Arthur gave to me right before he died? Well, they slid behind the stereo," Mrs. Hudson said.

Juliet glanced at the clock. "Oh. Do you need me to fetch them for you?"

"No, dear. I grabbed them," Mrs. Hudson said.

Juliet frowned. "Well, good."

"But then the stereo dropped on my leg," the elderly woman said.

Juliet sprang to her feet. "What? Are you all right? Do you need an ambulance?"

"Oh, no, dear. I'm fine. Well, not fine. My foot is bruised, and I can't stand on my tiptoes." Mrs. Hudson sighed.

"Do you need me to bring bandages or, well, anything?" Juliet asked.

"No. But I do need you to come and get my yellow bowl—the one with flowers on it—off my top shelf. I can't reach that high, and I'm going to Betty Adam's for Bunko tonight," Mrs. Hudson said.

Relief flooded Juliet. "I'd be happy to help. In fact, I could use a walk right now. Give me a minute."

"Thank you, dear." The elderly lady hung up.

Juliet chuckled. Now that was a confusing conversation. She slid her arms into her coat and headed for the door. "Deputy Phillips, I take it?"

Phillips nodded a buzz-cut head. He stood to about six feet and was built like a truck. "Yes, ma'am."

"How do you feel about a walk?" she asked.

"You walk, I follow, ma'am," he said with a smile and twinkling brown eyes.

"Excellent." She stepped into the chilly day and frowned at the gathering clouds. Not another heavy summer storm. She hustled down the block to Mrs. Hudson's white bungalow. She knocked on the door. The elderly lady hollered for her to come in.

Juliet left Deputy Phillips on the porch and hurried inside. "Mrs. Hudson?"

"In the kitchen, dear," Mrs. Hudson said.

Juliet removed her coat, entered the sparkling clean kitchen, and stopped short. "Quinn."

"Juliet." He sat at the round table, a large bowl of oriental chicken salad set on the crocheted tablecloth in front of him.

Juliet raised her eyebrows at Mrs. Hudson.

The woman smiled and pushed Juliet onto the chair across from Quinn. "The sheriff was kind enough to fetch my bowl, but now I need a couple of testers for the salad I want to take tonight." She dumped another bowl of oriental chicken salad in front of Juliet and smoothed her purple, velour pantsuit. "Now you two eat up, take notes, and I'll be right back. I promised Henry Bullton next door some salad." Humming to herself, she skipped out the back door.

Juliet's stomach knotted. "I thought she'd injured her foot."

Quinn took a bite of the salad. "Nope. She's interfering."

Juliet's hand stopped halfway to the fork. "Interfering?"

"Yep." He took another bite. "The word around town is that we broke up, and apparently, the news doesn't sit well with Mrs. Hudson."

Heat climbed into Juliet's face. "Well, it sits just fine with me."

"Does it, now?" Quinn polished off his salad. "Good to know." He stood—a strong man with a hard jaw. "I have a meeting in five minutes. Please tell Mrs. Hudson that I enjoyed the salad very much and to mind her own business."

"You tell her that." Juliet lifted her chin.

"I will." He halted at the kitchen door. "Make sure Deputy Phillips is with you all day, Juliet. I'd hate to fire the guy." Whistling a smart-ass tune, the sheriff sauntered out of sight.

CHAPTER 17

A raging headache set up camp behind Quinn's left eye as he shoved open the door to the station. While he adored Mrs. Hudson, he didn't need help figuring out his life. He needed time.

The silence in the station shot his blood pressure into overdrive.

Stopping at the reception counter, he pinned Mrs. Wilson with a hard look. "What's going on?"

"Don't you speak to me in such a tone, young man." She shoved her glasses up her pointy nose, giving him the same glare she had when he'd stolen tulips from her garden to give to a girl. He'd been eight.

He fought the urge to shuffle his feet. "I apologize, Mrs. Wilson. Why is it so quiet in here?"

"I think everyone is upset about this." She flashed a sympathetic grimace and slid the Missoula paper across the counter.

Dread dropped into his gut. He turned the paper around to see a front-page picture of him helping Juliet out of the truck at the funeral. The caption read: "Sheriff Lodge Escorts mob-daughter Juliet Spazzoli."

He scanned the article. Some of it touched on his reelection bid, but most of the article detailed the DEA's case and offered speculation about Juliet's crime family. Quinn handed the paper back to Mrs. Wilson. "Throw the entire thing away, would you?"

"Will this hurt you in the election?" she asked.

"I don't know." Right now, he didn't have time to worry about the election. As he entered the main hub of the station, all of a sudden, everyone was either on the phone, typing, or out of sight. With a sigh, he stalked between people who wouldn't meet his gaze until entering his office.

"We could sue the paper." Jake sat in a guest chair playing *Angry Birds* on his phone.

"Why? Most of the article seemed to be somewhat factual." Quinn skirted his desk and dropped onto his chair.

Jake shot another red bird into the air. "You'll need to campaign now."

"I don't have time." Quinn shoved papers out of the way.

Jake clicked his phone shut. "Do you want to be the sheriff or not?"

Right now? "Not."

"Liar." Jake stuck his phone in his pocket. "I've booked you on two radio stations next week. The interviews will go quickly, and you need to do them."

"Fine."

Jake grinned. "You and Juliet make up yet?"

"No," Quinn said.

"Stop being such a stubborn bastard," Jake said without heat. His eyes darkened with sympathy.

"She lied to me," Quinn grunted.

"Yeah. People make mistakes, Quinn. Even you." Jake cleared his throat. "Officially, I'm here to report that my client will testify to anything she has knowledge of regarding Freddy Spazzoli's drug business in exchange for both state and federal immunity."

Quinn lifted an eyebrow. "Does your client know anything she hasn't already shared?"

"Er, no." Jake grinned.

"Then not only is her testimony useless, she doesn't need immunity." Quinn doubted the DEA would waste time prosecuting Juliet without any proof.

The grin disappeared. "I still want the immunity. The money concerns me...and there's a decent accessory-after-the-fact charge if the DEA wants to make an example out of her. Push your friend for the deal, Quinn," Jake said.

"Dealing with the DEA is your job, Jake." Quinn settled back in his chair. He didn't deserve to be sheriff if he called in special favors. "You might also want to concentrate on the possession of false identification charge that will be heading Juliet's way soon. The local prosecutor will love the case."

"What false identification?" Jake asked.

"She brought false ID from New York to Montana," Quinn said.

Both of Jake's dark eyebrows rose. "Did she use any identification?"

"Don't know." Quinn crossed his arms.

Jake picked at his faded jeans. "Have you either seen this identification or applied for a warrant to search her home or place of business?"

Quinn scowled. "Obtaining a warrant is on the agenda for today."

Jake flashed the smile that made other attorneys quake. "Feel free. You won't find any identification."

Quinn gripped his desk. "You told her to destroy evidence?"

"Of course not. I didn't tell her a damn thing." Jake stood.

"Tell me you didn't destroy evidence," Quinn said, his breath heating.

Jake loped toward the door. "I believe I'll take the Fifth on that one, Sheriff. Have a nice day."

"You're an officer of the court," Quinn bellowed after his disappearing brother. Son of a bitch. The relief sliding through him pissed him off more. Exhaling, he started punching in letters on his keyboard. Those reports wouldn't write themselves.

An hour passed and someone tapped on his opened door. The scent of wild citrus hit him right in the solar plexus. Smoothing his face into interested lines, he focused on the door. "Hello, Juliet." Standing like his mama had taught him, he gestured her into a chair.

She gracefully crossed and sat. Her pale face and trembling hands made him feel like an ogre.

"How can I help you?" He retook his seat before he could grab her up and cuddle her close.

Her forehead creased. "I, ah, well, you requested my presence."

He leaned forward. "Who called you?"

"Mrs. Wilson." Juliet glanced at the door, no doubt seeking a quick exit.

"Mrs. Wilson?" Quinn yelled.

The file clerk poked his head inside the office. "Mrs. Wilson took a half-day sick day, Sheriff."

"I'll bet she did," Quinn muttered. He rubbed his whiskers. Had he forgotten to shave again? "I'm sorry, Juliet. Apparently I need to fire my receptionist."

"You're not going to fire Mrs. Wilson," Juliet said, her lips tilting slightly. "Anyway, I wanted to say how sorry I am for the newspaper article. I wish I could do something about it."

"Not your fault." Her scent was driving him crazy.

The file clerk returned to place a box on Quinn's desk. "From Shelby's bakery." The kid disappeared, shutting the door behind himself.

Quinn frowned at the box and flipped open the lid. Inside

lay several cookies, all shaped as hearts and decorated with a Q + J.

Juliet covered her mouth, her eyes lighting with amusement. "You have got to be kidding me."

Quinn cleared his throat. If the old biddies in town thought they could force him into anything, they were freakin' crazy. "I'm sorry about this, Juliet. Their interference is ridiculous."

She lost her smile. "I'm sorry, too." She rose, looking small and fragile.

He stood. "I, uh, am probably going to get a warrant to search your place later for the doctored identification." Damn it. He had no right to warn her.

"Oh." She tugged open a monstrous purse and rummaged inside. "I'll give the identification to you now."

"No." He hadn't wanted to set her up. Not at all. "Don't do that."

"No more hiding, and no more lies, Quinn. Take the ID. I bought it off a guy in the Village." She yanked out a wallet and searched through each slot. "I don't understand."

Relief dropped him back onto his seat. "Don't tell me—it's gone?"

"Um, yes." Juliet frowned. "I don't understand."

"I do." He shook his head. While part of him strongly disapproved, the other part wanted to buy his brother a drink later. As a thank you. "You should probably talk to your lawyer. Either way, there's no reason to search your place."

She turned toward the doorway. "Very well. Good-bye, Sheriff."

"'Bye, Juliet."

The door shut behind her with a sad sense of finality. Quinn Lodge glared at the cookies. What now?

ALTHOUGH EARLY, the country-western bar was already hopping. The band blared a quick tune, and several couples two-stepped across the sawdust-covered dance floor. Juliet eyed the clear liquid in the shot glass from her table near the bar. "I'm not sure doing shots is such a good idea."

Sophie shrugged and sipped her ginger ale. "Why not? I wish I could."

Anabella Rush tipped back her head and downed her shot. "Yeah. Why not?" Then she sputtered, her eyes watering.

"That's why," Juliet said slowly. What the heck. She grabbed the glass and poured the heated alcohol down her throat. The liquid rushed down and exploded in her stomach. She gasped and coughed.

Sophie smacked her on the back. "There you go, girlfriend. Now, did Quinn eat one of the heart-shaped cookies?" Her laugh competed with the band.

Juliet flushed. "Not while I was in his office. They just ticked him off." She sighed. "I don't think he'll let anybody push him into forgiving me. This whole plan by the town is going to backfire."

"I told Loni that." Sophie's eyes widened, and she slapped a hand over her mouth. "I mean, I, uh—"

"Loni's in on this?" Juliet gasped.

"Yep." Sophie nodded. "She likes you. A lot."

That was just sweet. Her heart warmed. "Well, that's nice." Juliet brushed sawdust off the table.

The fast song stopped, and Dawn Freeze stepped up to the mic to sing a country ballad. The entire place quieted. Low and sexy, the young woman's voice crooned around the room, creating a cocoon of intimacy. Several couples slid onto the dance floor.

Juliet leaned forward. "Wow. She can really sing."

"Yeah." Sophie grinned. "The guys hate her singing in a bar. Jake keeps trying to get her to sing more in church."

Considering his little sister was wearing tight jeans and a black half T-shirt that showed very smooth skin, Juliet imagined none of the brothers liked it much. Her gaze caught on a man across the bar watching Dawn with heated green eyes. "When did Hawk get back to town?"

"Last night. He's on leave for a week." Sophie turned as Colton plunked down a beer in front of Hawk. "Oh, great. There's our babysitter."

Juliet waved. "Don't be silly. He's here to hang out with Hawk and watch his sister."

Sophie frowned. "Colt can multitask, believe me. Darn protective Lodge-Freeze men."

"I miss my husband." Anabella hiccupped. She motioned to the waitress. "Another round, Milina."

Juliet's eyes widened. "Oh, I forgot to tell you. I went into my purse to give Quinn the false identification stuff I bought in New York, and it was gone. I have a terrible feeling my lawyer did something he shouldn't have done."

Sophie snorted and reached for her newly delivered plate of nachos. "That was me, girlfriend."

Juliet gaped. "Destroying evidence is illegal."

"So my rather angry husband explained in great detail when I told him what I'd done." Sophie reached for the bowl of pretzels. "Though, he kind of looked relieved, too."

"He yelled at you?" Anabella gasped.

"Nope. I'm all pregnant and delicate, you know?" Sophie grinned.

Juliet shook her head. "You broke the law."

"Prove it." Sophie's smile turned a bit lopsided. "No proof, no crime."

Anabella took another shot and sputtered. "Remind me not to tick you off."

Sophie nodded. "Yeah. Don't tick me off. I know stuff."

For some reason, all three women thought that was ridiculously hilarious. Their laughter brought interested looks from both Colton and Hawk. Sophie gestured toward them in what could only be called a smart-assed wave.

They laughed harder.

JULIET SIGHED DEEPLY right around midnight. "I think I'm too sad to get drunk."

Sophie sighed heavily. "Not me—I miss drinking."

"I'm not drunk." Anabella rubbed her nose. "But I can't feel my nose."

Sophie patted her hand. "You don't need your nose tonight."

"True." Anabella nodded wisely. "So true. But when my husband gets home next month, I hope I can smell him. He always smells so good."

Juliet sighed and scooted out of the booth. "I think it's time for water." She headed over to the bar and skidded through sawdust. Regaining her balance, she stopped short as a woman stepped in front of her. "Amy?"

Amy Nelson nodded, her gaze sweeping Juliet's jeans and boots. "Nice outfit, career killer."

"Thanks." Juliet glanced down at Amy's short skirt and vested top. "You look like a high-priced hooker." Oops. Maybe the alcohol had affected her.

Amy put both hands on her ample hips. "Why are you still in town? Time to leave."

"Why?" Juliet asked.

"Because you're already ruined Quinn's chance of being sheriff again," Amy said.

Juliet struggled to maintain a polite smile. "I don't think so. Quinn will still win."

"No he won't." A fierce smile split Amy's face. "Which is all right and in the plan. With all his money and all his charisma, the man could go much higher than sheriff, if he had the right partner directing him."

Juliet snorted and then covered her mouth in embarrassment. Taking several deep breaths, she clasped her hands. "Quinn doesn't take direction from anybody."

"I admit I've had to be careful. But now that he's out of the sheriff race, he can enter the Senate race next year. I'd love to live in DC." Amy frowned at Sophie and Anabella as they laughed back at the booth. "I'll have to get him out of this podunk town and away from his family. They are definitely holding him back."

Anger danced spots in front of Juliet's eyes. "Wait a minute. You're the one who alerted the Missoula paper?"

"Yep." Malicious glee danced in Amy's eyes. "I can't tell you how helpful you've been."

"This conversation is over." Juliet lifted her head and turned to sidestep Amy.

The woman dug sharp nails into Juliet's arm. "Get out of town before I destroy you even more than I already have."

"Let go of me." Juliet used her most regal voice.

Amy dug deeper and then shoved.

The world disappeared. Temper roared through Juliet so quickly she staggered. Clenching her fist, she swung and nailed Amy right in the jaw. The woman flew into the bar and slid down to the floor.

The front door opened to reveal the sheriff.

Juliet's eyes widened. Fists bunched and slightly drunk, she stood over the sheriff's ex-lover after having just clocked her one.

Oops.

CHAPTER 18

*J*uliet ended up in the same jail cell as last time. The wool blanket on the one cot shifted as she settled against the concrete-block wall. Quinn had taken one look at the scene in the bar and handcuffed both Amy and her. Handcuffed!

About an hour had passed before Quinn appeared on the other side of the bars. Even with anger warming her chest, her gaze ate him up. Tonight he'd donned faded jeans, scuffed cowboy boots, and a long-sleeved, dark green T-shirt. He'd tucked his gun at his waist, and the deadly weapon looked right at home. A deep shadow covered his jaw, and pure irritation shone in his black eyes.

She lifted her chin and refused to talk first.

"How's your hand, slugger?" he asked.

She crossed her arms. "Fine."

"Good. Amy Nelson has decided not to press charges." Quinn wrapped his hands around the bars.

Juliet lifted one eyebrow. "Really? That's surprising."

"Not after I explained that witnesses saw her push you before you laid her out, and that if I arrested you, I'd have to arrest her, too. I doubt the governor would appreciate bad press right now."

If the floor would open up and swallow Juliet, she'd be fine. "So, I'm free to go?"

"Maybe." The sheriff didn't twitch, apparently in no hurry to allow her out of the cell. "When I asked you to help out Anabella, I didn't mean to get her drunk and then get into a bar fight."

"I'm aware of that fact, Sheriff. I do apologize for my part in the disaster that became our night out." She stood. "Now, unless you feel I deserve more jail time, I'd like to go home."

His eyes darkened. "What you deserve is a good walloping that keeps you from sitting for the next week."

Her head jerked up. Nails bit into her palm when she clenched her already aching fist. "I do beg your pardon."

"Oh, you'd beg." He stepped closer to the bars. "Enough of the nonsense, Juliet. I don't have time to chase you all over town, break up bar fights, and drive home drunk women who cry the entire time because they miss their husbands. Either promise you'll behave, or I'm leaving you in the cell for the night."

Her spine straightened one angry vertebra at a time. "While I know you have no reason to believe me, most of those issues weren't my fault. Now either let me out, or allow me to call my attorney."

He kept her gaze, and she fought the very real urge to step back. Finally, with an irritated male sigh, he unlocked the door and slid the bars open. "I'll drive you out to Jake and Sophie's. They're waiting for you."

"No, I—" Her protest caught in her throat at the flare of anger in his eyes. "That would be fine. Thank you." Frankly, she didn't want to go home alone.

He escorted her out of the station and to his black truck, waiting until her seat belt had been fastened before pulling out of the parking lot. They drove in silence through town and toward the reservation.

The moon caressed his rugged face, enhancing his hard jaw and full mouth. Every once in a while, his Native heritage stood out in primitive relief. Tonight was one of those nights.

Her glance caught on his large, capable hands on the steering wheel. "Sorry you have to drive me home." His grunt in response had her rolling her eyes. "Your sister is an amazing singer."

"Humph." Quinn glanced out at the clouds rolling across the moon.

Fine. The sheriff didn't want to talk. Juliet shoved hair out of her way and glanced at the darkening forest outside as the moon disappeared. Thunder rumbled in the distance. The sky crackled and opened up. Rain pelted the truck.

Quinn flipped on the windshield wipers with a flick of his wrist. "Are you warm enough?"

"I'm fine." She hugged herself with her hands and chastised herself for not wearing a coat.

A cop's gaze raked her head to toe. Without saying a word, he increased the heat. "Stop being stubborn."

"Me, stubborn?" She glared at him. "You're the most stubborn person I've ever met."

His cheek creased.

Suddenly, he veered the truck toward the trees. Swearing, Quinn hit the brakes and yanked the wheel. Only his quick reflexes kept them from hitting a huge lodgepole pine. They rolled to a stop. Quiet descended.

He eyed her. "You okay?"

"Fine." Except her heart might've been bruised from beating so hard against her rib cage. "What happened?"

"Deer. I want to make sure I didn't clip him." He jumped out of the truck and into the rain.

Clunks sounded from the back. Quinn shone a bright light

into the forest. Juliet released her seat belt, leaped from the truck, and hurried toward the sheriff.

Quinn looked over his shoulder. "Get back in the truck."

"No." She stepped gingerly off the road. "Two pairs of eyes are better."

He wiped rain off his forehead. "Juliet, the rain is freezing, and this will just take me a minute. Now get your ass back in the truck."

"I am so finished taking orders from you, Quinn. Kiss my butt. Twice."

He barked out a laugh and turned to shine the light into the trees. No animal stared back. With a shrug, he turned and was on her before she could take another breath. Hands on her hips, he lifted her easily, walking backward until he'd opened the door and plopped her on the seat.

Enough was enough. She kicked out with all the frustration and anger she'd stifled for days. And nailed him right in the thigh.

They both froze for a second. She opened her mouth to apologize, but he was faster. He pulled her toward him, his mouth smashing hers with what must be the anger and frustration *he'd* stifled for days.

Sharp teeth nipped her bottom lip, and she opened her mouth in surprise.

He dove in.

Gone was the congenial sheriff and the gentle lover. In his place stood a primitive man she wanted more than her next thought. His fingers threaded through her hair held her in place. His hips kept her legs apart, and his mouth took what he wanted. No finesse, no kindness, just pure, raw lust.

Sharp pangs of need ripped through her. Her body ached. She moaned deep in her throat.

He released her, his eyes blazing. "If you want to stop, tell me now," he rumbled.

"I don't want to stop." She ripped open his shirt, needing to feel him. All of him.

His free hand grabbed the bottom of her shirt and hauled it over her head. The second the flimsy material was free, his mouth took hers again. One flick of his finger released the front clasp of her bra, and his hand, calloused and demanding, palmed her breast. Her nipples peaked. He tweaked one, and she whimpered with raw need.

He released her hair and grabbed her jeans with both hands. The button zinged against the windshield, and the zipper ripped free. Strong hands dragged off her boots, the jeans, and her panties. Jerking down his jeans, he gripped her ass, lifted her, and impaled her.

She gasped in shock.

He was too big...too much.

Rain slid down his torso, and she rubbed her hands into the wet hardness.

He stood in the rain, at home in the dangerous storm. Droplets pelted him, matting his hair and dripping over the hard angles of his face. Hard hands kept them groin to groin. His easy strength in bearing her weight cascaded tingles through her abdomen. Hot and sexy, those tingles had nothing on the flaring nerves where his cock stretched her.

His gaze pinning her, he ran one hand up her spine to secure the back of her neck. Then he lifted her and plunged her back down along his length. His groin slid against her clit.

Spikes of pleasure rippled from where they were joined. Her mouth opened wide on her exhale.

A satisfied smirk creased his face.

Need and want shot through her. She grabbed his shoulders to lift herself, to get him moving.

The hand on her hip and the one at her nape prevented her movement. His watchful gaze kept her captive as he stood in the storm, holding her. Controlling them both. Then he waited.

Determination sharpened his cheekbones, hardened his jaw. The man would wait until day broke.

Something feminine stretched awake inside her. She took in the dangerous warrior, seeing him finally for the primal being he was at heart. The sheriff tempered his wild nature with good humor and a protective embrace encompassing the entire community. For the first time, she glimpsed the predator inside.

Feminine instinct took over. She smoothed her palms on his shoulders and relaxed her body. Relaxing into his strength, to his will, she allowed him to take her wherever he wanted to go.

A masculine gleam lightened his eyes.

He shifted until they both stood in the rain, her back to the truck. Then he thrust inside her, pounding with a ferocity wilder than the storm. The coolness of the water contrasted with the heat from the male taking her, throwing her into a maelstrom of sensation. The hard pounding, the chilled rain, the warm man, the love bursting through her heart…swirled together until her mind shut down.

His fingers gripped her hips, his hard shaft pounded inside her, leaving his mark as completely as he'd left his brand in her heart.

With a cry of his name, she broke. Splinters of shooting pleasure cut through her, and she rode them out, lost in the sensations. He ground against her with his own release. Her orgasm lasted forever. Finally coming down, she relaxed against him. He held her tight.

Quinn walked them back to the open truck door and set her gently on the seat.

Her heart clutched. Not a word had passed between them. Without looking at him, she grabbed her shirt off the steering wheel and scooted over to the passenger side.

What now?

JULIET FROWNED at Sophie sitting across the scarred wooden table in their booth. The scents of grease and burned toast coated the air. "I don't care how bad your cravings are. I shouldn't be out in public today."

Sophie rubbed her baby bump. "Come on. Leila is at Loni's, and I needed a greasy breakfast from the Dirt Spoon. Nobody will recognize us here."

Juliet shook her head. "I appreciate you letting me stay the night, but we should've remained at your house for breakfast." In fact, they'd promised Colton they'd do just that so he could go help mend the fences. He'd declared they had enough ranch hands around that if either woman called for help, several people would be up from the barns instantly.

Instead, they'd headed to town. "I feel guilty about this," Juliet murmured. "I'm sure we're safe, but still. We did promise Colton." Although, not much could happen to them in the middle of Mineral Lake. Seriously.

"The guys had to fix fences after the storm last night. It was easy to get away so we could talk." Sophie studied her. "You were rather disheveled when Quinn dropped you off last night."

Disheveled and heartbroken. The sheriff hadn't said a word after handing over her clothing and dropping her off. Well, nothing but an order to stay at Jake and Sophie's until he fetched her the next day. "I don't want to talk about it," Juliet muttered.

Sympathy curled Sophie's lip. "I understand. I'm married to a Lodge, remember?"

"Yes, I know. But Quinn and I aren't married. Heck, we're not even talking." Sure, he'd mounted her like she was a prize mare the previous night, but without talking, there was no intimacy. "I could just shoot him."

"Been there, seriously considered doing that." Sophie took a deep drink of an herbal tea before grimacing. "Shooting Jake, I mean. I never wanted to shoot Quinn. Until now." Loyalty lifted her lips in a sweet smile.

"I've probably broken enough laws lately," Juliet said wryly. "I'll be right back." She headed to the restroom, filing through the room filled with several people she'd seen at the bar the previous night.

She reached the door, and the hair on the back of her neck prickled. Slowly turning around, she already knew who she'd see.

"Morning, JJ," Freddy said.

She took a breath to scream and halted as he drew a gun. A shiny, almost too big for his hand, silver gun. It wavered.

"You have a choice." Freddy glanced toward the busy restaurant. "Either come nicely with me, or I'll take both you and your pretty friend. Please, JJ. I just wanna talk to you."

"Go where?" She edged toward the bathroom. If she could get inside, maybe there was a lock.

"My partner would like to discuss the missing millions with you." Freddy grabbed her biceps. "Please. It'll just take a minute." Desperation creased his forehead.

"There's no money," she admitted.

"Nobody is stupid enough to give away that kind of money." He swung her around and dug the gun into her ribs. "If you want, you could make a lot of money with us. You'll need to relocate and start over, but hey, you're good at pretending to be someone you're not." Kicking a back door open, he pulled her into the chilly morning air.

"Fine. I'll go with you." She could scream and struggle, but there was a good chance the gun would go off. Even if the idiot didn't shoot her, he might shoot somebody else. It'd be a lot easier to jump out of a moving vehicle when he drove past the police station. She'd been so stupid to leave the damn ranch. However, she'd always been able to handle her half-brother. She could deal with this situation easily. "Let's go, Fred."

"Thank you. I promise, you'll be happy you did." He dragged her around the corner to the alley. "I can't believe how clean the alleys are in this stupid town. Who has clean alleys?"

"I think it's a county ordinance." She stumbled over a puddle, splashing mud on her jeans. "You know the sheriff is going to skin you alive for this, right?" Quinn might not like her any longer, but a woman kidnapped in his county would truly anger him.

"Jesus, JJ. The guy fucks you, and you think he's invincible?" Freddy's hold tightened. "He's a stupid hick—one who'll end up dead if he comes after you."

"Who's your partner, Freddy?" She eyed the end of the alley. Maybe she could trip him and make a break for it.

"Oh, you'll meet him. He's got some real good ideas for making money," Freddy said.

A black SUV slid into the alley, and a man jumped out. Much bigger than Freddy, the guy wore guns in a shoulder holster, leg holster, and at his waist. He reached them in two strides. Dead blue eyes stared into hers. "Where's my money?"

The moment changed from an irritating one with Freddy to a deadly one she might not escape. Her mouth went dry.

A truck sped by the other end of the alley.

The guy tugged something from his pocket. He grabbed her hands and zip-tied them, pulling too tight. She bit her lip to keep from giving him the satisfaction of knowing he'd hurt her.

Getting in the car would be disastrous. She jerked away and opened her mouth to scream. He manacled her around the waist and yanked her into his body, slamming a hand over her mouth. She struggled, kicking and twisting, but he hauled her to the car and tossed her in the back, where she smashed into another man. The first jumped in beside her. "You drive, Fred."

"No problem, Luis." Freddy lifted himself into the front seat and put the truck in drive.

Trapped. Her hands bound, she sat between two large men. Screaming seemed like a good idea. She sucked in air—

"If you scream, I'll have to knock you out," Luis said calmly.

She paused. If he rendered her unconscious, she wouldn't be able to get away. She glanced at the man on her right. Several scars lined his face, and he kept his gaze on the buildings outside. Guns and knives were tucked into his pants and leather vest. A man in the front passenger seat was similarly armed and also keeping watch of the world outside.

She swallowed. "You guys going to war, or what?"

Luis chuckled. "No. We have a shipment coming in and like to be prepared."

Freddy drove through the archway to town and turned the vehicle toward the mountains. The safety of the city of Mineral Lake disappeared behind them. Hopefully they'd remain in Maverick County.

She had to get out of the vehicle. Somehow.

CHAPTER 19

*T*he cabin smelled like mildew. Juliet twisted her wrists. The zip-tie dug into her skin, holding tight. Luis had pushed her into the cabin and chair thirty minutes ago, and her arms had gone numb. So much for her big escape plan.

A chill from the wooden chair swept up her spine, and she eyed the small area. The place was more of a shack than a cabin. A rough fireplace took up one wall, a dingy kitchen the opposite. In the middle sat a round table with four rickety chairs. One wall held doors to what looked like a small bedroom and bathroom. The final wall showcased a medium-sized window that probably had a decent view of the mountains behind the soiled blue blanket covering the panes. Her laptop perched on the table, humming softly.

Luis nodded to Freddy. "Go scout the south perimeter while I chat with your sister."

Dread settled in Juliet's gut.

Freddy stilled and then eyed Juliet. With a sympathetic grimace, he nodded and dodged outside, shutting the door.

Luis grabbed a large envelope off the table and twirled it with long fingers. End over end. Again, end over end, his gaze on her, thoughtful and somehow more menacing than if he were angry. "Where's my money?"

"The money I found in my trunk is long gone." She met his dark scrutiny without flinching.

He drew a picture from the envelope to toss in front of her. The photo depicted Quinn standing on the steps of the sheriff's station, his eyes narrowed, his body alert.

"I believe the sheriff has excellent instincts." Luis pulled out another picture. "He apparently felt me watching. However, had I decided to shoot him, his instincts wouldn't have helped." With a twist of Luis's wrist, the next photo landed on the table.

Juliet barely kept from gasping. The new picture showed little Leila and a pregnant Sophie walking hand in hand out at Sophie's ranch. "You spent some time taking pictures."

"I like to be thorough." He yanked out several pictures to throw on the table. Pictures of Juliet, pictures of townspeople, pictures of her friends. "I could've ended the life of any one, or all, of these people at any time. And I will."

She slid her most polite smile into place. "I believe you."

"Good. Where's my money?" Luis asked.

"I'm telling you the truth," she said evenly.

He drew a wicked-sharp knife from his back pocket. "You have a very pretty face."

"That's kind of you to say." She might throw up now.

He grinned. "While I enjoy a complete smart-ass, I will cut you."

Her stomach knotted, but she kept his gaze. "That doesn't change the fact that the drug money is long gone."

His eyes hardened. He skirted the table and slid his hand around her throat, lifting her head and squeezing just enough to make breathing difficult. "I'm losing my patience."

She swallowed through the constriction. If he moved a little to the left, she could knee him in the groin—she'd have one shot. Somehow, she had to get him out of his head. So she focused on him and...winked.

He blinked. Admiration slid into his gaze. "I'm really regretting we couldn't go into business together, Juliet."

Surprise slid through her. "Freddy said you had another plan to use my business as a front."

Regret twisted Luis's lip. "You were set up perfectly in Maverick to front my operation. Unfortunately, when you went clean with the sheriff, you destroyed any chance of our working something out."

"Oh," she murmured. "So if I tell you where the money is, I'm pretty much finished."

"You're a lot smarter than your brother," Luis said.

"The doorknob is smarter than Freddy," she muttered.

Luis threw back his head and laughed, the sound slightly maniacal. "I like you. A lot. So here's the deal. Tell me how to find my money, and this will go smoothly." He leaned in, his minty breath brushing her skin. "If you don't cooperate, I'll hurt you like you can't imagine."

Bile rose up her throat, but she shoved it down. Her smile hurt. "I'm not that tough, Luis. I promise." If she gave him the file in her computer that showed where all the money had gone, he'd kill her. If she didn't give it to him, he'd torture and then kill her.

His hold loosened. "I'll help you decide. If I have to work at getting the information, when I'm finished with you, I'm going to start on the people in those pictures. Probably with pretty Sophie Lodge. I usually prefer blondes." He tucked his face into Juliet's hair and took a deep breath. "Though maybe I'll switch to redheads."

She gagged.

He backed away, irritation bracketing his mouth. "Tell me the truth."

Her mind scrambled for a way to stay alive. "Did you kill the two men on the outskirts of the county?"

Luis shrugged. "They tried to steal from me, and a man does have to keep control of his employees."

Luis liked to talk, and for some reason, he seemed to enjoy talking to her. She had the oddest feeling he wanted to impress her. Well, before he tortured her. "Did you kill them with that knife?"

His smile flashed sharp teeth. "Juliet, you don't seem to understand that there's no need to gather evidence for your boyfriend."

The mention of Quinn pricked tears at the back of her eyes. "I was just curious."

He slid the knife closer to her face. Light glinted off the sharp blade. "Yes, this is the knife." His voice dropped to a croon. "Isn't she pretty?"

Wow. Whackjob.

The door banged open, and Freddy stalked inside with a tall, skinny man who had more pocks in his skin than freckles. And he was seriously freckled.

"The first shipment is here." Freddy glanced at Juliet, his shoulders relaxing.

Had the moron been worried about her? Not worried enough to stop Luis, though. Juliet glared at the weasel.

Luis jerked his head toward the bedroom. "The money's in the green duffel."

Freddy hustled into the bedroom and returned to hand the duffle to the freckled guy. "It was a pleasure."

The man left without saying a word.

Freddy rubbed his hands together. "One more shipment, and we're out of here."

Juliet cleared her throat. "You know, Fred, I've noticed Luis doesn't seem tolerant of employees screwing up."

Freddy frowned. Luis smiled. Juliet tried to keep from puking.

Freddy eyed Luis and then focused on her. "And?"

"You screwed up. You lost his money, and now you lost his chance to use my gallery as a front. Frankly, I'm shocked you're still standing." She tilted her head toward the deadly knife. "Something tells me you'll be rather intimate with that blade in the near future."

Luis chuckled. "I swear to God, Fred, I think I'm in love with your sister." He twirled the knife like a gunslinger playing with pearl-handled pistols. "Look at her try to cause a rift between us. She's stalling, and I find it adorable." His gaze raked her down to her boots. "Though if she doesn't tell me where the money is, I'm going to kill her."

Freddy stilled. "Tell him, JJ. He promised not to hurt you if you just told him."

Juliet shook her head. "You're such a moron. He lied to you."

Freddy's mouth opened and shut like a guppy out of water. "No, he didn't. You're safe. I promise."

"He's going to kill you, too, Fred. Get a grip," she said.

Luis tucked away the knife and drew a gun, pointing it at Freddy. "I'm done. Tell me where the money is, or I shoot him."

"What the hell, man?" Freddy backed away, both hands up.

Luis flipped off the safety. "I'm counting to three."

Juliet's brain scrambled.

"One," Luis said calmly.

"T-tell him, JJ," Freddy sputtered.

"Fine." She didn't want to see Freddy's brains splattered all over the wall. "I kept track of where the money went. The document is called 'Robin Hood' in my laptop."

Keeping the barrel aimed at Freddy, Luis punched keys with his left hand. His eyebrow lifted as he seemed to read. "You gave all of my money away...to Lost Cats of Spokane?"

She shrugged. "I only gave them ten thousand. But those cats needed catnip, Luis."

His eyes widened, and his pupils narrowed. Shifting his aim from Freddy to her, he drew back his lip. "You're going to pay for this in ways I can't even imagine right now."

∾ ∾ ∾

HIS BACK TO A PONDEROSA PINE, Quinn shook his head at his brother. "We can't wait for backup."

"I know," Colt said grimly, yanking off his work gloves. "You armed?"

"No—except for a pocket knife in my boot." Quinn eyed the shotgun secured in a holster on Colton's horse. "I think that's it for guns."

Hawk shoved through the brush to the secluded area. "There are four men patrolling, plus whoever's in the cabin." Nodding toward a ridge to the north, he rubbed his chin. "That area has vantage over the valley—should take me five minutes to be in place. I'll need Colt's shotgun."

Quinn took a deep breath to keep from running full bore toward the cabin. "Hawk, we've never talked about—"

"I'm a sniper. The best." Hawk's odd-colored green eyes darkened.

That's what Quinn had figured. "Okay. Take the northern ridge."

Jake shoved his way past the bushes, a wicked knife in his hand. "I took this off the guy patrolling to the east."

"Is he dead?" Quinn asked calmly.

"No. Out cold." Jake tucked the knife at his waist. "I sent Sophie back to town, although she wanted to stay and help."

The little blonde had seen Juliet kidnapped and had followed in her car, calling the guys on her cell phone. Quinn's gut swirled. "Thank God we were working on the northern pastures."

Hawk tilted his head. "I'm heading to the ridge. Give me five." He loped over to the tethered horse and yanked the shotgun free. With a grim look at Colton, he broke into a jog and disappeared from sight.

Quinn peered around the tree at the quiet cabin. A heated ball of dread slammed him. Was Juliet all right? What if they'd hurt her? His legs trembled with the need to storm the cabin.

Jake grabbed his arm. "Give Hawk a moment to get into position."

Quinn grunted. "She thinks I'm still mad at her."

Colton removed his jacket. "You are."

"Doesn't mean I don't still love her." Sure, he'd been a complete asshole and should've worked things out after he fucked her by the side of the road. But he was a stubborn bastard, and his anger had kept him silent. If anything happened to her, he might as well shrivel up and die.

"Get it together, Sheriff." Jake's eyes darkened with concern and anger. He cared about Juliet, too.

Drawing on years of experience, Quinn shoved emotion out of the way. Cold, methodical, he came up with the campaign to save the woman he loved. The plan held definite risk, and likely somebody would be shot, but it was all they had.

"Let's go," he said grimly.

❦ ❦ ❦

JULIET EYED the man who wanted to harm her. Her mind buzzed, but her shoulders relaxed. She must be in shock, which wasn't so bad.

Luis twirled the knife. "The good news is that I'm not going to kill you right now. The bad news is that you're coming with us, and I'm going to take my time with you tonight." His eyes lightened to a creepy leer.

Juliet lifted her chin regally. The longer she stayed alive, the better the chance of escape. "Sounds like a lovely plan."

The window shattered, and a large mass crashed through the blanket. Quinn! The door banged off its hinges a second later, and Jake barreled into the room followed by Colton.

Luis pivoted and shot toward the window.

Juliet screamed.

Quinn rolled into a somersault and cut Luis off at the knees, knocking him down. The gun spun across the floor. The men grappled, their punches landing hard.

Jake grabbed Freddy and shoved him face-first into the wall.

Colton viewed the bedroom and bathroom. "Clear," he said.

Blood flowed from a wound in Quinn's right shoulder. Luis shoved his knuckles in the injury.

Quinn hissed and elbowed Luis in the nose, following up with a cracking uppercut.

The drug dealer shook his head, snot and blood pouring from his nose. He punched Quinn hard in the wound.

The sheriff grunted, his face paling. His damaged arm hung limp by his side.

Luis smiled through bloody teeth and yanked back his fist.

Quinn dropped his head forward in a classic headbutt. Luis's nose broke with a terrible snap. He howled in pain. He grabbed Quinn's arms and fell onto the floor, throwing the sheriff over his head.

Quinn landed with a muffled curse.

Juliet's gaze darted to Jake and Colton, where they calmly watched the fight. What was wrong with them? Why weren't they moving to help?

Quinn rolled to his feet and came down hard on Luis, banging the man's head on the floor. With a grim smile, the sheriff flipped Luis onto his stomach, straddled and cuffed him.

"Are you all right?" Quinn turned toward her, his eyes hard and assessing.

She nodded, unable to speak. Tears swelled and blurred the room.

Quinn yanked Luis to stand and pushed him toward Colton. "Secure them in the back of the gray truck."

Luis chuckled through a split lip. "I have men around the perimeter, Sheriff. Let me go, or we're all dead."

"We found your men." Quinn wiped blood off his forehead. "My sniper is in place in case we missed anyone. I'll bet my sniper against your guys any day."

Luis spit blood and a couple of teeth onto the floor. Colton grabbed him and shoved him outside.

Jake pulled Freddy away from the wall and smashed him back into it. "Oops," Jake said, grinning and tugging again. "Come on, buddy. Let's go outside." They disappeared into the cold.

Quinn reached her in two strides. "Are you sure you're all right?"

"Yes," she said between hiccups.

"Take it easy, sweetheart." He tugged a knife from his boot and cut the tie holding her hands. Then he glared at her scratched skin, rubbing gently.

"I'm fine," she said, standing. Her knees gave out.

He eased her back into the chair. "Take a couple of deep breaths. The adrenaline is kicking in now." Big, gentle hands massaged her legs and then her shoulders. "You're fine, Juliet. Deep breaths."

She nodded and inhaled, exhaling slowly. "How did you get here?"

"Sophie saw Freddy take you." Quinn dropped to his haunches. "I almost had a heart attack when she called. We were just a couple miles away working on a downed fence and headed right here."

She sniffed. "I'm glad you did." Her eyes widened at the blood coursing down his arm. "He shot you."

Quinn frowned and ripped his shirt over his head. A deep, red gash welled on his upper arm. "The bullet scratched me. No biggie." He wrapped his shirt around the wound and pulled tight.

Sirens sounded in the distance. He grimaced. "I'm sorry about last night. I was a jerk who couldn't figure out what to say."

She blinked through tears. The man had just saved her life after she got him shot, and he was apologizing. "This is my fault." The sirens got closer.

He stood and assisted her up. "We called for backup." Not that Quinn needed backup.

Juliet squared her shoulders and slid her feet along the wooden floor. Her knees still wobbled. "I'm sorry about all of this."

He dropped a kiss on her forehead. "I know. We'll figure it out, Juliet. I promise."

When they reached the doorway, she peered outside. "Um, do you really have a sniper somewhere?"

"Hawk was with us fixing fences." Quinn gave some weird military sign. "Don't worry. He rarely shoots the wrong person." A grin quirked the sheriff's lip.

"Very funny." She gingerly stepped onto the muddy walkway. Red-and-blue lights swirled as deputies gathered several cuffed men into police vehicles.

A black SUV screeched to a stop, and Reese Johnson jumped out. "Is she all right?"

"Yes," Quinn said, helping her along the rough trail to a police vehicle. "Did you get the drug runners?"

Reese grinned. "Yep. We caught one with a shitload of cash and another one with a truck full of drugs." He nodded at Juliet.

"I've gotten the okay to offer you full immunity for everything if you testify as to what you witnessed today."

Jake shoved away from a police car. "While my client doesn't need immunity because she hasn't broken any laws, we would still like the offer in writing from the federal prosecutor."

"Sheriff Lodge? Over here." A camera light flicked, and a man with a microphone stepped closer. "What happened here?"

Quinn moved toward the reporter.

"Stop." Jake grabbed his arm and hitched him back. He opened the back door of a cruiser and reached for Juliet's hand. "Get in." Juliet scooted over, and Quinn dropped next to her.

Jake smiled. "I'll meet you two at the hospital."

Quinn moved to get out of the car. "I want the reporter out of here."

Jake leaned in. "I called him, dumbass. Trust me." After shoving his brother, he slammed the door.

A deputy slid behind the wheel. "To the hospital we go, Sheriff."

CHAPTER 20

Juliet leaned her head against the chilly wall and tried to get comfortable on the plastic orange chair. Even in quaint Maverick, the hospital smelled like bleach, antiseptic, and despair.

The doctors had rushed Quinn into a room upon their arrival, and a petite but rather forceful nurse had directed Juliet to the waiting area. In the corner, a television played an old sitcom.

Her stomach hurt. She closed her eyes, allowing peace to wash over her. Everybody was safe, and the bad guys had gotten what they deserved.

What about her? What did she deserve? She sat up as Quinn's mother hustled into the room.

Loni Freeze gathered her into a vanilla-scented hug. "Oh my goodness. You worried me." She patted Juliet's back, offering maternal comfort.

Tears welled in Juliet's eyes. She leaned away and blinked. "I'm fine, but Luis shot Quinn."

"I poked my head in the examination room. Quinn is barking orders at the poor doctor." Loni shook her head, sending her gray braid flying. "That boy. I don't know where he gets such a temper."

Tom Freeze, Loni's husband, rushed into the room with Dawn. "I know exactly where he gets his spirit." He dropped a kiss on Juliet's head. "I'm glad you're all right, sweetie." Then he sat and slipped his hand over Loni's.

As a pair, they fit. Tall with gray hair and deep blue eyes, Quinn's stepfather contrasted with Loni's black eyes and sharp features.

Dawn was a perfect blend of the two, with blue eyes and black hair. Those eyes lit up when Hawk and Colton stalked into the room.

Juliet clasped her hands. "Thank you. Both of you."

They nodded.

Dawn frowned. "I didn't know you helped rescue Juliet, Hawk."

He shrugged. "I provided backup and let the sheriff do his thing."

Did Dawn not know Hawk was a sniper? Juliet raised an eyebrow. The young man met her gaze evenly, without expression. Her small nod promised she wouldn't tell.

Sophie ran into the room next, skidded to a stop and tugged Juliet out of her chair for a big hug. "I was so worried. I saw Freddy take you, and I didn't know what to do, so I followed in my car and called the guys for help, but if I didn't get them, I wasn't sure what—"

Juliet hugged her hard. "Take a deep breath. Thank you, and I'm fine."

Sophie stepped back and surveyed Juliet head to toe. "You look all right."

"I'm fine." She forced a smile. "Quinn got shot, not me."

Colton nodded toward the television. "Is this your doing, Jake?"

The film clip showed Quinn escorting Juliet out of the cabin amid deputies arresting the drug runners. Reese Johnson stood next to the reporter, thanking the Maverick County Sheriff for assisting with the biggest drug bust in recent history. He claimed justice was served only because Juliet Spazzoli put herself in danger to help authorities.

Jake grinned. "Someone has to make sure the sheriff gets reelected. Can you imagine if he worked the ranch full time?"

"No. He's bossy enough as it is." Colton gave an exaggerated shiver.

Hawk slowly nodded. "Amen."

Jake rubbed his chin. "I think the DEA will offer a deal to Freddy, Juliet. Just so you know."

A relief that made her feel guilty swept through her. "I know I shouldn't be, but I'm glad."

Jake's eyes filled with understanding. "Family is still family."

The room started to crowd with concerned citizens and police officers. Excusing herself, Juliet stepped outside. She figured she'd walk home and do some thinking, as well as make herself some lunch. Shouldn't she be hungry? Perhaps the next day she'd talk to Quinn.

Did childhood insecurity hold her back?

A deputy smoked outside his car. "Ms. Montgomery? Would you like a ride home?" He tossed the cigarette into a mud puddle and opened the back door. "The sheriff would kick my butt if I let you walk home with a storm coming."

A chilly wind swept through her thin sweater. With a grateful nod, she slipped into the warm patrol car. "Thanks."

The deputy glanced over the seat. "This way the sheriff will know where to find you when the doc is finished stitching him up." At his cocky grin, he pulled the car into the road.

Juliet rolled her eyes. Now even his deputies attempted to matchmake. If they only understood that nothing swayed the stubborn sheriff. Nothing.

❧ ❧ ❧

JULIET STRETCHED HER ARMS, much more comfortable in her yoga outfit. She'd changed the second the deputy had dropped her at home. It was a good thing she'd accepted the ride, considering her knees had started trembling within seconds of sitting down. Apparently the adrenaline rush took a while to dissipate.

Flipping on the local radio station, she tried to relax.

The empty apartment mocked her. She should eat lunch, but nothing seemed appealing right now.

Her heart ached an actual, physical, thumping of pain. Oh God. She was truly, absolutely, completely in love with Quinn Lodge.

She wondered how Quinn was doing. Maybe she should've stayed at the hospital.

Shame heated her face. The guy had taken a bullet for her, and she'd fled because she was too chicken to talk to him. She'd run away. Like always. Too afraid he'd reject her.

But she'd needed to get away and think...the same way Quinn had said he needed time to think.

Maybe he wasn't finished with her—he just had needed a second to breathe.

A broadcaster interrupted a Garth Brooks song with an update about the sheriff being shot and a promise that there would be a press conference in a few minutes. Sheriff Quinn Lodge would be outside the sheriff's building shortly.

He'd gone back to work? After being shot? Irritation heated her skin. The man needed a keeper. In fact, he needed her. Her head jerked up. She didn't want to run again. Not from him. In fact, she wanted to keep him. To fight for him. The decision flowed through her, straightening her spine.

Sure, she'd lied to him—and she'd been stupid not to trust him. But everyone made mistakes.

He'd said he loved her.

People who loved each other forgave each other. Look at the meddling, pain-in-the-butt town. Everyone tripped over everyone else.

But they forgave each other. Because they loved each other.

Quinn Lodge was a good man—a good man who should be fought for.

Juliet Spazzoli could be heck of a fighter.

She ripped open the outside door and stomped into the early evening. If the sheriff thought he could just screw her and dump her, then he was as stupid as Freddy. As she reached the curb, she almost collided with Mrs. Hudson and Henry Bullton.

"Well, hello, dear." Mrs. Hudson smiled, her powdered skin wrinkling. "Henry and I wanted to drop by and see if you'd like to go for a walk." She pushed Juliet toward the sidewalk.

Henry nodded, his green puffer jacket two sizes too large over his bony body. He'd obviously put mousse in his thin gray hair because it spiked up all over. "The sheriff is about to give a talk." Sliding a bony arm through Juliet's, he tugged her away from the door.

Two uniformed deputies jogged over from Kurt's Koffees.

Juliet stumbled. "Deputies Phillips and Baker? Are you looking for me?"

"Yes, ma'am," Deputy Baker said. "We grabbed coffee and were headed to your place to escort you to the press conference." He elbowed Deputy Phillips, who just shrugged.

Juliet frowned. "How did you know I planned to attend?"

Phillips grinned. "We didn't, but we thought we might talk you into it."

She narrowed her gaze. "I appreciate the support, but—"

A SUV screeched to a stop, and Sophie, Loni, and Dawn hopped out.

Dawn hustled over to assist Mrs. Hudson. "Oh, good. We thought we'd have to drag you to the sheriff's station, Juliet."

Juliet dug in her heels. "Why are you all pushing me there?"

Loni smiled. "I love my boy, but he's a stubborn one. He's hurt, you're hurt, and there's no time like the present to fix things."

Sophie skipped over a mud puddle. "Plus, he won't exactly yell at you in front of cameras. Well, probably only one camera. But still."

Juliet's mind spun as the group herded her down the street. They passed several blocks and picked up an even bigger crowd. Finally, they arrived at the sheriff's office.

Quinn stood on the top step, wearing a clean shirt and jeans. Several reporters and one cameraman had set up in front of him. His wet hair curled over his collar. His eyes were hard, his jaw set, and his shoulders impossibly wide. Slowly, one dark eyebrow rose when he noticed her.

She stepped closer to him. "Can we talk?"

The camera swung to her.

"Now?" A crease deepened between his eyebrows as he took in the gathering townspeople.

Loni nudged Juliet up the rest of the steps.

She steeled her spine. "I'm sorry about getting you shot." There. She'd said it.

Jake slid into view. "I believe the sheriff would like to thank you for your help in setting up the drug dealers, Juliet." Several people in the crowd nodded.

Quinn loomed over her with an intimidating stance, apparently not giving a hoot about the election, cameras, or crowd. "You forgot to apologize for disobeying me and ending up in danger. I told you to stay at Jake's until I picked you up today."

She glowered. "I don't take orders from you, Sheriff." Her gaze caught on the white bandage peeking out of the neck of his shirt. "Though I am truly very sorry you were shot." She winced.

"What part of 'Don't leave Jake's until I come and get you'

did you not understand?" He was mad. Beyond mad. Fury filled the sheriff's eyes...fury at her.

Jake interjected again. "The woman wanted to help you catch a drug dealer. She's a hero."

The crowd roared with a chorus of, "She's a hero."

Good Lord. She swallowed. "I know. But you're not perfect, either."

His gaze softened. "I know, and I really am sorry about last night."

"What happened last night, Sheriff?" a reporter asked.

Juliet's face heated.

Quinn glared at the reporter. "None of your damn business."

Juliet put her hands on her hips. A feminine instinct she hadn't realized she had awakened. Determined. Ready to fight if necessary. Fight with him. More importantly—fight for him. He was everything she could ever want in this life...or the next. She leaned up and whispered into his ear, "You said you loved me."

"I do love you. Why didn't you tell me the truth?" he whispered back. Something besides anger flashed in his eyes. Hurt. She'd hurt him.

"We can't hear you, Sheriff," a reporter called.

"No shit." Quinn lifted his voice.

The crowd rustled. A photographer flashed pictures.

Juliet leaned into him. "At first, you were just the hard-core sheriff, and I didn't know you. Then, when we became close, I'd already lied for so long. I didn't want to lose you. Didn't want to disappoint you." She kicked her foot and watched a pebble roll away. "I'm sorry."

"Look at me, Juliet," he ordered.

The low tone tingled through her body. Gathering her courage, she looked him right in the eye. "I really am sorry."

"Do you love me?" he asked.

"Yes. I love you," she said easily.

"No more lying?" he asked.

Hope bloomed in her chest. "Only honesty from now on. I promise."

"I love you, too." He brushed a curl off her cheek. "I planned to head to your place after this stupid press conference."

Tingles lifted her smile. "You were?"

"Of course. I'm not letting you get away, Juliet." He tugged her close, and his mouth took hers.

The spectators erupted in cheers.

EPILOGUE

Quinn parked the truck against a lodgepole pine, looking dashing in a black shirt and faded jeans. Maybe not dashing, but definitely handsome and stronger than the mountains around them.

"My stomach is in knots." Juliet smoothed down her skirt.

He glanced toward Loni and Tom's sprawling ranch house. "Either I won or I lost and will run for sheriff next time. If I lost, I wouldn't mind working the ranch a little harder. The guys seem to be slacking a bit."

Juliet smiled. "You're overbearing."

His cheek creased. "So you've told me."

"Thank you for helping me with the DEA." She'd gotten immunity for anything she might have done and had supplied affidavits against Freddy and Luis. Freddy had made a deal to testify against Luis in exchange for a lenient sentence. Luis had pled out since the evidence was so strong.

The criminal issue was over.

Unfortunately, maybe Quinn's career was, too.

He slid from the driver's seat and crossed around to open

her door. After assisting her to the ground, he shut the door. "I thought this would be a nice place to chat."

She wobbled in her new boots. "Chat? Are you stalling, Sheriff? Let's go inside to the party and see if you've been reelected or not."

"Yes, chat." He shuffled his feet and cleared his throat. "My family means a lot to me and will always be in my business and in my life."

"Okay," she said.

"So will the town, the reservation, and the entire county." He tugged on his already open collar. "You need to understand my life."

Where in the world was he going with all of this? Perhaps he felt more nervous about the election than he'd let on, but he wasn't telling her anything she didn't know. Of course his family and the town would always be a part of him. "I do understand."

"Good." He breathed out, relief lightening his eyes. "In that case"— he dropped to one knee and yanked a small box out of his pocket— "will you marry me?"

The world stopped spinning. Completely stopped. Nothing moved, nothing breathed. Juliet froze, her mind blank. Her knees quivered.

Quinn opened the box to reveal a spectacular square diamond surrounded by intricate Celtic knots—all in platinum. It was the most beautiful ring she could've ever imagined, offered by the most amazing man on the planet.

Her breath whooshed out. Birds sprang to a loud chirping. The wind rustled around them. Joy filled her so completely she swayed. "Yes."

Relief filled his eyes followed by a huge smile splitting his face. "Yes." He slid the ring on her finger and stood, gathering her close for a kiss that started sweet and ended deep.

A roaring filled the early evening. They broke apart to find his family, deputies, and half the town spilling onto the porch.

"Woohoo." Loni clapped her hands. "Get out the posters."

Several 'Congratulations on Your Engagement' posters and banners instantly were taped along the house by many pairs of willing hands.

"How did you know?" Quinn drew Juliet closer to the crowd.

Leila shook her head. "Uncle Quinn. Just 'cause you bought the ring in Billings don't mean we don't know people there." She smiled, revealing a gap in her front teeth. "Duh."

"Yeah, duh." Jake reached out and shook his brother's hand before enfolding Juliet in a hug. "Welcome to the family."

Hugs, kisses, and congratulations surrounded them until everyone finally piled back inside. Quinn held Juliet's hand, keeping her on the porch. "Life is going to get crazy, sweetheart. My job doesn't have normal hours, and I'm involved in more than just keeping order."

She smiled, running a reassuring hand down his arm to gaze up at his dark eyes. "I know, and I like being part of the community. Besides, I still get free rent at the gallery, right?" Her lips curved as amusement filtered through her. She was already planning another art showing for Sophie.

He chuckled. "Well, how about I let you *earn* free rent?"

"Hmmm. Sounds kinky." Turned out Juliet liked kinky. Who knew?

"You know the whole pretending-to-date plan was a setup to get you right where I wanted you?" He brushed a kiss across her nose.

"Maybe you ended up right where I wanted you." She levered up on her toes and slid her lips along his. "You're everything I could ever want."

Quinn tucked her closer and took over the kiss, going deep. They both breathed heavily when he released her.

Jake poked his head outside. "Preliminary numbers are in.

Looks like you're the sheriff again." He turned back toward the party. "Damn it, Colton. That was my plate of nachos." He disappeared from sight.

Quinn tangled his fingers with Juliet's. "Well, sweetheart? Welcome to chaos."

She grinned and walked with him into the family home and into a chaos where she belonged. "I like it here."

"Good thing." His hold tightened. "I love you, Juliet."

She leaned into his strength. "I love you, too." There would be no more running. She'd finally found her home.

❧ ❧ ❧

IF YOU LIKED Quinn's story, read Colton's story next in Rising Assets . Here's a quick excerpt:

"She can't be working here. No way." Colton Freeze leaned forward in his chair and slid his nearly empty beer on the battered wooden table. A jukebox belted out a Garth Brooks melody, peanut shells lined the floor, and longnecks took residence on almost every table in the bar. Unfortunately, the sense of home failed to relax him.

"I'm only telling you what Mrs. Nelson said at the bank." His friend, Hawk, turned toward the long, oak bar. "If she is working here, I wish she'd show up so I can go home to bed."

"Soon." Colton shook his head. "There is no way Melanie works at the coffee place in the morning, her ranch all day, and Adam's bar at night." She hadn't bothered to tell him. He'd been overseas finishing his securities degree, and nobody had thought to tell him his best friend was working herself to death? A fear he hadn't experienced in over ten years, when she'd become ill with pneumonia, slammed him between the eyes, nearly bringing on a migraine. He shoved the sensation away.

"I didn't know, or I would've called." Hawk gazed thoughtfully across the smoky room, his odd green eyes narrowed.

"You've only been home a day." Colt frowned. He cocked his head as the bartender called into the kitchen with a, "Hi, Mel."

Unbelievable. She *was* working at the bar. Colton steeled his shoulders and schooled his face into a pleasant expression. If he yelled at her right off the bat, she wouldn't talk to him, and that would get him nowhere.

He needed to speak with her. While they'd grown apart a little bit during their teenage years, when they'd moved on into the world, they'd kept in touch as he attended school. After her grandfather had died two years ago, they'd reconnected, and Colton had made sure to call, text, and email while he studied.

After a short time, he couldn't sleep without talking to her and sharing his day. Maybe he should've been home instead of pursuing knowledge.

As his best friend, she was needed. He'd almost lost her once to the pneumonia, and he'd never allow himself to feel such fear again. She'd been what? Maybe twelve years old? From that day, he and Hawk had always made sure she had a coat nearby, although she hadn't gotten sick again. Now his gut churned that she hadn't shared her problems with him. "Where in the world is she?" he muttered.

She emerged from the kitchen and stepped out from behind the bar. Colton straightened in his chair. "What the hell?"

Hawk emitted a slow whistle. "Wow."

Yeah, wow. Melanie's customary outfit of faded jeans, scuffed boots, and farm perfect T-shirt was absent for the night. "Adam must have made her wear the outfit." Son of a bitch. He'd kill the bar owner.

Hawk leaned forward, elbows on the table. "She looks good."

She looked better than good, and shock sprang Colt's cock into action. A tight tank top showed off perfect breasts, while a skirt curved along her butt to stop a couple of inches away. Long, lean legs led down to high-heeled boots. She was a wet dream come true.

Melanie wobbled a full tray of drinks to deliver to a table of rowdy farmers.

"Maybe the medical bills from her grandpop's fight with cancer added up, and she needed the extra money?" Hawk rolled his shoulder and finished his beer.

Colton exhaled but couldn't look away from the sexy brunette. Sexy? Jesus. It was just the shock of the new look. She was still Mel, still his best friend. "Now I need to worry about both of you."

Hawk sighed. "Tell me you didn't ask me out for a beer my first night home to lecture me."

Colton turned toward his oldest friend. Lines of exhaustion fanned out from Hawk's eyes, and a dark purple bruise mottled his left cheekbone. He was usually battered when he returned home from active duty, but this time a hardness had entered Hawk's eyes. Now wasn't the moment to bug him, however. Colton shrugged. "Nope. Just wanted to catch up. I'll push you tomorrow on leaving the SEALs."

"Fair enough." Hawk took a deep swallow of his beer as his gaze remained on Melanie. "I'm glad you called. It appears as if things might get interesting tonight."

Doubtful. Colton turned his attention back to the woman who hadn't trusted him enough to let him know she was in trouble. Something in his chest ached, and he shoved the irritant aside with anger. While he was known for a slow-to-burn temper, especially in comparison with his two older brothers, when he exploded, it was legendary.

There would be no temper tonight. First, he had to figure out what was going on, and then he had to solve the issue. Logically and with a good plan. When Mel glanced his way, he lifted his empty glass.

She hitched around full tables to reach him. "Why did you cut your hair?" Her face was pale as she tried to tug her skirt down.

He knew she wouldn't be comfortable half nude in public. "When did you start waitressing in a fucking bar?" The words slipped out before he could stop them.

"Smooth," Hawk muttered into his beer.

Melanie arched a delicate eyebrow and released the bottom of the skirt. "Last I checked, my grandfather was dead and you weren't my keeper. Do you want another beer or not?" The tray hitched against her hip—a hip that wasn't nearly as curvy as it had been the previous year. She'd lost weight.

Even so, he wanted to grab that hip and... "What time do you get off?" he asked.

A dimple twinkled in her cheek. "It depends who I take home with me."

He couldn't help but grin back. "You are such a big talker."

"I know." She shoved curly brown hair away from her face. Hair wild and free. "Why are you asking? Think you'll need a ride home?"

"I'm taking you home, and we're talking about your three jobs." He tried to smooth his voice into charming mode, but the order emerged with bite.

"The last time you tried to boss me around, I hit you in the face and you cried for an hour." She nodded at a guy waving for a drink from a table on the other side of the dance floor.

Colton glared at the guy. "I did not cry."

"Did too," Hawk whispered.

Colton shot a look at his buddy before focusing back on Mel. He'd been seven years old, and she'd almost broken his nose. "My eyes watered from the punch. That wasn't crying." They'd been having the argument for nearly two decades, and the woman never let up. "You've cried on my shoulder many a time."

She reached for his glass. "That's because men are assholes, and you have great shoulders."

Every boy or man who'd ever hurt her had ended up bashed

and bloody afterward because either he or Hawk had made sure of it. "You're right on both counts. Which begs the question, if you're in trouble, why aren't you crying on my shoulder now?"

Sadness filtered through her deep eyes. "You're my friend, not my knight. It's time I stood on my own two feet."

He wanted to be her knight, because if anybody deserved protection, it was Melanie. "I'm mad at you."

"I know." She smacked his shoulder. "You'll get over it. You always do."

Was it his imagination, or did regret tinge her words? He tilted his head and studied her.

She smiled at Hawk. "I'm glad you're home. You staying this time?"

Hawk lifted a shoulder. "We'll see. It's nice to be among friends, I can tell you that."

Mel fingered Colton's short hair, returning her attention to him. "Why did you cut it?" she asked again.

That one touch slid down his spine and sparked his balls on fire. What in the hellfire was wrong with him? He shifted his weight. "I thought it was time for a more mature look since I'm taking over at the office." Of course, last time he'd grappled at the gym, his opponent had gotten a good hold on Colton's hair. At that point, a clipping had become inevitable.

Mel smiled. "You do look all grown up, Colt Freeze."

He'd love to show her just how grown up. At the odd thought, he mentally shook himself. Friend zone. Definite friend zone. That was it. "Part of being a grown-up is asking for help."

She rolled her eyes. "I'll be back with another beer." Turning on a too-high heel, she sauntered toward the back corner.

Colt's gaze dropped to her ass. The flimsy skirt hugged her flesh in a way that heated his blood. While Mel was small, she had always been curvy. More than once, he'd wondered.

For years he'd gone for wild girls...fun, crazy, and not

looking for forever. During his life, he'd avoided anything but friendship with Melanie, who was a keeper. A good girl, sharp as a blade, and kindhearted.

Hawk cleared his throat.

"What?" Colton asked.

"You're looking at Mel's butt." Hawk set down his beer. "How long have I been out of town, anyway? Has something changed?"

Colton shoved down irritation. "No. Besides, what's wrong with Mel's butt?"

"Nothing. In the world of butts, it's phenomenal." Hawk leaned to get a better view. "Just the right amount of muscle and softness. In fact—"

"Shut up." Colton jabbed his friend in the arm. Hard. "Stop looking at her ass."

Hawk chuckled. "If you're finally going to make a move, let me know. I have a hundred bucks entered in the town pool."

Colton's ears began to burn. "Town pool?"

"Yep. The exact date you and Melanie finally make a go of it." Hawk pushed back his chair. "Now that you're home, get ready for some meddling."

"Mel and I are just friends." He'd kill himself if he ever hurt her. In fact, he beat the crap out of her first boyfriend in high school because the prick had cheated on her. So the fact that she had an ass that made Colton's hands itch to take a hold of was something he'd ignore. Again.

"I may stay home for a while, because this is going to be fun." Hawk stood. "Mind if I head out? I need sleep."

Colton shook his head. "No problem." Hawk did require sleep if he was thinking Colton and Mel could be anything more than friends. The three of them needed each other, and things had to stay the same. "I'll see you at your southern pasture at dawn. The order of twine finally came in earlier."

"Can't wait." Hawk turned and headed out of the bar, seemingly oblivious to the several pairs of female eyes tracking his progress.

A voluptuous pair of breasts crossed Colton's vision before a woman plunked down in Hawk's vacated seat. "Well, if it isn't Colton Freeze," Joan Daniels said before sliding her almost empty wineglass onto the table.

"Hi, Joan." Colton forced his gaze to her heavily made up eyes and away from the twins being shoved up by a bra worth twice whatever the woman had paid for it. "How are you?"

Joan pouted out red lips. "Almost empty."

"We'll have to get you another." Colton slid a polite smile on his face. While he may be single and definitely horny, he was far from stupid. The four times divorced cougar leaning toward him represented a complication he neither needed nor wanted. Talk about not fitting into his plans. "Are you out by yourself tonight?"

"Yes." She clasped her hands on the table and shoved her breasts together in a move as old as time. "How about you since Hawk took off?"

"I'm waiting until Melanie is off shift." It wasn't the first time he'd used his friendship with Mel as an excuse, and it probably wouldn't be the last.

Joan sniffed. "Why? She's still dating the oldest Milton son from Billings, right? The banker?"

Colton lifted a shoulder. If Mel was still dating the banker, it was the longest relationship she'd ever had. The idea shot a hard rock into his gut, one he'd have to figure out later. His unease was probably due to the fact that any banker wearing three-piece suits and allowing his woman to work three jobs wasn't good enough for Melanie. Though using the word *allow* around her would end in a broken nose. Colton smiled at the thought.

Melanie slid a beer in front of him and leaned over to pour wine into Joan's glass.

Joan narrowed hard eyes. "How did you know what kind of wine I want?"

Melanie recorked the bottle. "You're drinking red. *This* is our red."

Colton bit back a grin. Adam's wasn't known for a fine wine selection, but beer was another matter. "Did you bring me a nice beer?" He glanced closer at the thick brew. "Looks hearty."

"Suck it up and try the new beer, wimp." Mel nudged his shoulder.

Joan leaned closer to Colt. "We were discussing you and Brian Milton."

Melanie eyed Colton. "Is that a fact?"

The tone of voice held warning and had the unfortunate result of zipping straight to Colton's groin. He felt like a randy teenager all of a sudden, and enough was enough. "I wasn't." If all else failed, throw the cougar under the bus. "Joan brought up Milton."

"Why?" Melanie turned her formidable focus onto Joan.

"Curiosity." Joan's caps sparkled even in the dim light. "You've been dating for quite a while. Is it serious?"

"It's personal." Melanie dropped a couple of beer napkins on the table. "I have a ride home, Colton."

"Yeah. Me." He took his drink and gave her his hardest look —one that wouldn't faze her a bit. "Either agree, or there's gonna be a memorable scene in the parking lot when I toss your butt in my truck."

Sparks flashed in Melanie's eyes. She leaned in, and the scent of lilacs and woman almost dropped him to his knees. "Threaten me again, Freeze, and I'll make you cry for hours."

He'd never been able to refuse a challenge, so he turned his head until their lips hovered centimeters apart, his gaze piercing hers. "Sounds like a date."

Order Rising Assets Today!

SERIES' LIST

I know a lot of you like the exact reading order for each series, so here you go as of the release of this book, although if you read most novels out of order, it's okay.

MONTANA MAVERICK SERIES

1. Against the Wall
2. Under the Covers
3. Rising Assets
4. Over the Top

KNIFE'S EDGE, AK SERIES

1. Dead of Winter
2. Thaw of Spring

THE ANNA ALBERTINI FILES

1. Disorderly Conduct
2. Bailed Out

3. Adverse Possession
4. Holiday Rescue novella
5. Santa's Subpoena
6. Holiday Rogue novella
7. Tessa's Trust
8. Holiday Rebel novella
9. Habeas Corpus

LAUREL SNOW SERIES

1. You Can Run
2. You Can Hide
3. You Can Die
4. You Can Kill

GRIMM BARGAINS SERIES

1. One Cursed Rose
2. One Dark Kiss

DEEP OPS SERIES

1. Hidden
2. Taken novella
3. Fallen
4. Shaken novella (in Pivot Anthology)
5. Broken
6. Driven
7. Unforgiven
8. Frostbitten

Dark Protectors/Enforcers/1001 DN

1. Fated (Dark Protectors Book 1)

2. Claimed (Dark Protectors Book 2)
3. Tempted novella (Dark Protectors 2.5)
4. Hunted (Dark Protectors Book 3)
5. Consumed (Dark Protectors Book 4)
6. Provoked (Dark Protectors Book 5)
7. Twisted Novella (Dark Protectors 5.5)
8. Shadowed (Dark Protectors Book 6)
9. Tamed Novella (Dark Protectors 6.5)
10. Marked (Dark Protectors Book 7)
11. Wicked Ride (Realm Enforcers 1)
12. Wicked Edge (Realm Enforcers 2)
13. Wicked Burn (Realm Enforcers 3)
14. Talen Novella (Dark Protectors 7.5)
15. Wicked Kiss (Realm Enforcers 4)
16. Wicked Bite (Realm Enforcers 5)
17. Teased (Reese Bros. novella)
18. Tricked (Reese Bros. novella)
19. Tangled (Reese Bros. novella)
20. Vampire's Faith (Dark Protectors 8) *****A great entry point for series*****
21. Demon's Mercy (Dark Protectors 9)
22. Vengeance (Rebels novella)
23. Alpha's Promise (Dark Protectors 10)
24. Hero's Haven (Dark Protectors 11)
25. Vixen (Rebels novella)
26. Guardian's Grace (Dark Protectors 12)
27. Vampire (Rebels novella)
28. Rebel's Karma (Dark Protectors 13)
29. Immortal's Honor (Dark Protector 14)
30. A Vampire's Kiss (Rebels novella)
31. Garrett's Destiny (Dark Protectors 15)
32. Warrior's Hope (Dark Protectors 16)
33. A Vampire's Mate (Rebels novella)
34. Prince of Darkness (DP 17)

STOPE PACKS (wolf shifters)

1. Wolf
2. Alpha
3. Shifter

SIN BROTHERS/BLOOD BROTHERS

1. Forgotten Sins
2. Sweet Revenge
3. Blind Faith
4. Total Surrender
5. Deadly Silence
6. Lethal Lies
7. Twisted Truths

SCORPIUS SYNDROME SERIES

Scorpius Syndrome/The Brigade Novellas

1. Scorpius Rising
2. Blaze Erupting
3. Power Surging - TBA
4. Chaos Consuming - TBA

Scorpius Syndrome Novels

1. Mercury Striking
2. Shadow Falling
3. Justice Ascending
4. Storm Gathering
5. Winter Igniting
6. Knight Awakening

REDEMPTION, WY SERIES

1. Rescue Cowboy Style (Novella in the Lone Wolf Anthology)
2. Rescue Hero Style (Novella in the Peril Anthology)
3. Rescue Rancher Style (Novella in the Cowboy Anthology)
4. Book # 1 launch - subscribe to my newsletter for more information about the new series.

WHAT TO READ NEXT

I often get asked what book or series of mine people should read first. All books are in written in past tense except for the Grimm Bargains books, which are in present tense. All of my books, regardless of genre, have some suspense and humor in them—as well as romance, of course. They're all fairly sexy romances except for the Laurel Snow thrillers and the Anna Albertini Files.

ROMANTIC SUSPENSE SERIES:

Deep Ops:

This series is about a ragtag group of misfits at Homeland Defense that create a team with each member finding love during a suspenseful time. Each book features the romance of a different couple, told through multiple POVs. Their mascots are a German Shepherd who likes to wear high heels because he feels short, and a cat named Cat that likes to live in pockets and eat goldfish. The crackers, not real fish. Probably. The series starts with Hidden and continues on with new books being released every year.

Sin and Blood Brothers:

These seven books are about brothers created in a lab years ago who've gotten free while still being hunted by the scientists and the military man who trained them. They each find love and romance during a suspenseful time. Each book features the romance of a different couple, told through multiple POVs. The first four books are called the Sin Brothers and then the next three are a spinoff called the Blood Brothers. The series starts with Forgotten Sins.

The Scorpius Syndrome:

This is a post-apocalyptic romance series. A bacteria wiped out 99% of the human race. For survivors, it affects their brains, either making them more intelligent, sociopathic, or animalistic. Jax Mercury, ex-gang member and ex-serviceman, returns to LA to create an inner city sanctuary against all of the danger out there, while hopefully finding a cure. Each book is a suspenseful romance between two people told in multiple POVs. The first book is Mercury Striking. There are four prequel novellas called The Brigade, and the first one is called Scorpius Rising.

Knife's Edge, Alaska

These feature four brothers who've returned to their small Alaskan town in the middle of nowhere. Each book features the romance of one of the brothers along with a suspenseful situation that's solved by the end. The books are told in multiple POVs. The first book is Dead of Winter.

Montana Mavericks:

These books are set in Montana in a small town with a bit of suspense in each one. The romance is the focus of these, and there's some good humor. This is a band of brothers type of romance with a very involved and rather funny family. They'd be considered category romances and have dual POVs. The first book is Against the Wall.

Anna Albertini Files:

I wasn't sure where to categorize these stories. They lean more toward women's fiction or even chick lit, featuring small-town hijinks as Anna solves a new case in each story. She has a very meddling family and ends up in very humorous situations while solving cases as a lawyer. In the first book, it appears she has three potential love interests (but only ends up with one), and by the second book, the love interest is obvious and develops each book. Fans love him. This is told in Anna's POV in first person, past tense. The first book is Disorderly Conduct.

There are Christmas novellas as well, each featuring one of the Albertini brothers' romance, and these are told in multiple POVs and third person. The first Christmas novella is called Holiday Rescue.

Redemption, Wyoming Series:

This one features a group of men from around the world who were kidnapped and forced to work as mercenaries for years. They escaped and have made their way to Wyoming, trying to live normal lives as ranchers with a clubhouse. Their motto is: If it can be ridden, we ride it. (Meaning horses, snow-mobiles, motorcycles...LOL). So far, the three prequel novellas have been published, and they're each in an anthology. I should have a date for the series launching soon.

ROMANTIC THRILLER SERIES:

The Laurel Snow Thrillers

These feature Laurel Snow, who's an awkward genius and profiler now working out of her smallish Washington State home with a team - many readers love the secondary characters as well. There's a slow burn romance with Fish and Wildlife Officer Huck Rivers, and each book involves a case. There are different POVs in this one, and a really fun antagonist who readers love to hate. The first book is called You Can Run.

PARANORMAL ROMANCE SERIES:

The Dark Protectors

This series launched my career and is still going strong. The main characters are brothers who are vampires at war with other species. The vampires, demons, shifters, witches, and Fae are all just different species. They can go into sunlight, eat steak, and quite enjoy immortality. They only take blood in fighting or sex. There are fated mates, and once they mate, it's forever with a bite, brand, and sex. They can't turn anybody into a different species, so vampire mates don't turn into vampires, but the mating process increases a human's chromosomal pairs so they get immortality. The first book is called Fated. There's a spinoff that's really part of the main series, and the first book is called Wicked Ride. Then there's a great entry point for the series (a new arc) called Vampire's Faith. Each book in these features a new couple and is told in multiple POVs.

Stope Pack Wolf Shifters

This is a paranormal series featuring wolf shifters set in Washington state. It's sexy and fun. The first two books feature the same couple, and the rest of the books feature a new couple's romance. These are told in dual POVs, and the first book is called Wolf. Yeah, it's kind of on point. LOL.

DARK ROMANCE SERIES:

Grimm Bargains

This is a dark romance series featuring retellings of fairy-tales set in the modern world. Through time, four main families have learned to exchange health and vitality with certain crystals, and in today's day and age, they use these crystals to power social media companies. They have mafia ties. This series is in first person, present tense - told from various POVs. It's my only present tense series. It is dark (not hugely dark compared to some of the dark romances out there), so check the trigger warnings. The first book is called One Cursed Rose, and it's a dark retelling of Beauty and the Beast.

ACKNOWLEDGMENTS

Thank you to everyone who played a role in bringing this tale of love, danger, and redemption to life. If I've forgotten anyone, please blame the whirlwind of small-town intrigue—it's tough to keep track of everything when there's a mysterious past to unravel and crimes to solve.

First, a heartfelt nod to Big Tone, my steady hand and constant muse through every twist and turn. Whether we're watching sunsets on the back porch or debating plotlines over coffee, you're always my biggest supporter. Thanks for reminding me that home is wherever we're together—bonus points if there's a cowboy hat involved.

To Gabe, for proving time and again that balancing a full schedule and helping out when chaos strikes isn't just possible but inspiring. Your dedication keeps me grounded and motivated to keep telling stories. Thanks for always being there to lend a hand—or a laugh—when I need it most.

A round of applause to Karlina, whose creative spark knows no bounds. Your unwavering belief that art belongs everywhere —even in dusty backrooms and old barns—reminds me why this story about the intersection of passion and persistence had to be told. Thanks for sharing your magic and making the world (and my work) so much brighter.

Gratitude galore to Kathleen Sweeney and the talented team at Book Brush, not just for crafting a cover that perfectly captures the heart of this story but also for your incredible social media assistance. Your ability to bring my characters to life and help them find their audience is a gift I treasure deeply.

Thanks to Caitlin Blasdell, my literary agent and beacon of wisdom, for navigating the world of publishing with grace and clarity. You keep my stories sharp, my characters compelling, and my goals on track.

To Anissa Beatty and the Rebel Street team—your creativity and support make every step of this process easier and more exciting. Your talent is as boundless as the open plains of this story's setting.

Hats off to Kristin Ashenfelter, whose TikTok ingenuity helps connect these characters with readers far and wide. Your dedication to finding new ways to share stories is a modern marvel, and I'm grateful for every idea you bring to the table.

Special thanks to Gabi Brockelsby for taking the time to do a quick Beta read on this one. Your thoughtful feedback helped fine-tune this story, and I'm so grateful for your insight and support.

Thanks to Writerspace for spreading the word about this story of love, risk, and redemption, ensuring it reaches readers who long for a little suspense and a lot of romance.

To my family and friends—Gail and Jim English, Kathy and Herbie Zanetti, Debbie and Travis Smith, Stephanie and Don West, Jessica and Jonah Namson, Cathie and Bruce Bailey, and Chelli and Jason Younker—thank you for cheering me on at every stage of this journey. Your support is the rhythm to this story's heart.

Finally, to you, dear reader, for taking a chance on this tale of small-town intrigue and big emotions. I hope it leaves you with a sense of adventure, a smile on your face, and maybe even a soft spot for a certain cowboy sheriff and the art dealer who captured his heart. Thank you for making this journey possible —you're the reason I keep writing.

ABOUT THE AUTHOR

New York Times, USA Today, Publisher's Weekly, Wall Street Journal and Amazon #1 bestselling author Rebecca Zanetti has published more than eighty novels and novellas, which have been translated into several languages, with millions of copies sold worldwide. Her books have received Publisher's Weekly, Library Journal, and Kirkus starred reviews, favorable Washington Post and New York Times Book Reviews, and have been included in Amazon best books of the year.

Rebecca has ridden in a locked Chevy trunk, has asked the unfortunate delivery guy to release her from a set of handcuffs, and has discovered the best silver mine shafts in which to bury a body...all in the name of research. Honest. Find Rebecca at: www.RebeccaZanetti.com

Made in the USA
Monee, IL
07 April 2025